MISS ANNA'S FRIGATE

Jens Kuhn

Copyright ©Jens Kuhn 2010

All unauthorized copying or distribution is prohibited.

All rights reserved.

Second edition 2013
ISBN 978-1-4457-3317-3

Into the distance, a ribbon of black
Stretched to the point of no turning back
A flight of fancy on a windswept field
Standing alone my senses reeled
A fatal attraction holding me fast, how
Can I escape this irresistible grasp?

Pink Floyd

JENS KUHN

Many people have helped me with this book. I will explicitly mention just a few: Gudrun Ingemarsson for her knowledge about Swedish history, Melanie Sherman for her useful comments and adverbial forgiveness and Alex Blackburn for kindly agreeing to edit the second edition.

Jens Kuhn is a writer of steamy fiction, mostly with a historic theme. He has published three novels in print and several short stories as ebooks. On this blog you can find out more about his books and read some of his more steamy short stories for free

Jens lives with his wife, two stepchildren and a cat in an old drafty Victorian house with five fireplaces in the historic town of York, UK. He enjoys paddling his kayak and searching for free wood to keep his old house warm and cosy.

Before moving to the UK, Jens lived in Stockholm, Sweden for many years. During the summer months he used to sail his small yacht in the same waters where the action of this novel takes place.

Prologue

His Britannic majesty's frigate Tartar of 32 guns labored heavily in the steep seas of the Baltic winter storm. Ice cold spray drenched the few people of her crew whose duty did not permit them to seek the shelter of the galley – or any other place that was less wet, albeit not less warm. Many of the crew were sick, a fact that might seem strange considering that the ships and men of the Royal Navy were used to sailing in any weather and on any ocean on the planet.

But ships built to cross oceans in any weather, and men used to it, still can become affected by the unusual motion of the Baltic Sea. It is a small body of water and very shallow. It is this shallowness that makes the waves steep and choppy in a blow, a motion which can still make even a seasoned sailor's stomach queasy. Add the extreme cold of the Northern latitudes and the often poor clothing of the sailor – and you have a recipe that can easily get you into trouble.

In the great cabin, Captain Baker tried to keep himself from falling out of his chair while he read his latest orders once again. He had been on the Baltic station for almost a year now, sent here last spring when war broke out between Sweden and Russia.

Sweden, being Britain's ally in the seemingly endless struggle against the ambitions of Napoleon Bonaparte, needed help with the Russian high seas fleet. A British squadron had been sent and together with Swedish frigates and ships of the line they had managed to blockade the Russians in Estonia and essentially prevent them from throwing their weight into the fight.

Not that it made any difference. Sweden was losing the war anyway, losing it rapidly. During the summer of 1808 Russian troops had managed to occupy Finland. Now they were preparing for the winter campaign – probably just waiting for the ice to bridge the way to the Åland islands and the Swedish mainland. Captain Baker tried to imagine the sight of a whole army, thousands of men, marching over the ice just like that. Horses, gun carriages, everything. The thought was so strange to him that he had difficulty taking it seriously. But he knew it had been done before, in fact quite regularly.

Returning back to his orders, Baker frowned. He would be stuck here during the winter and he didn't like it. After a year of boring patrols and running errands for the bigger ships' captains he would have liked to return to warmer waters and get some real action. Perhaps the Mediterranean, or even the West Indies. Where the water was warm, the sun shining and the crew could work on deck without freezing to death. He called to the sentry at his door. "Pass the word for Mr. Reeman and Mr. Pope!"

"Gentlemen," Captain Baker said, once the first lieutenant and the sailing master had arrived, shivering from the short walk on the deck outside. "We have new orders, I am afraid."

"We are not going home then, sir?" Reeman's words were not really a question.

"No. Quite the opposite. We are to proceed to the Swedish capital, if the ice will let us, that is."

The sailing master looked startled. "And if it does not, sir?"

"Then we are to anchor as close to the place as possible, Mr. Pope."

"But why?" Reeman looked puzzled. "What can we do if we are all trapped in the ice and unable to move, sir?"

"I think," the captain answered thoughtfully, "that this is quite the idea, my dear fellow. The admiralty wants us to be stuck up here."

"But for what purpose?"

"In order to keep an eye on things, I dare say."

"Like spying, sir?"

"If you choose to put it that way, lieutenant. Now, plot me a course for the coast, Mr. Pope. Mr. Reeman, instruct the lookouts to keep an eye open for ice. Oh, and they are to be relieved every half hour – if they'll last that long at all in this cold..."

Chapter 1 – Winter Bliss

"Won't you come back to bed, darling?" Anna said softly. She was lying on her side, her head propped up by her left arm, looking at the naked back of the man who was in front of the fireplace on the other side of the room. He was stacking up pieces of wood, working efficiently. Anna admired the play of the muscles along his back.

"In a minute, dear, I just want to get this fire going. Aren't you freezing?"

Anna shivered. Of course she was freezing. This was Sweden in winter. She pulled up the sheet closer around her with her right hand.

"But the maid can do this, Eric." Anna smiled to herself hearing her own words. She had never had a maid in her whole life. She had never even lived in a house this big, and she still had difficulties believing it sometimes.

Anna Wetterstrand, well, at least this was the name she was still using after the events of last summer, had never been rich. Of course, she had met rich people before, she even had stayed over in a few castles – but that had been work, duty. She had enjoyed it, naturally, but she had always been aware that she was there, doing what she did, for a purpose not of her own.

Then she had met Eric af Klint, the young nobleman with his thin, wiry body, soft, clean hands and his very special nose. He had been gunnery officer aboard an inshore fleet gunboat that had delivered her to one of her missions, into Russian occupied Finland. He had also saved her life and touched her heart. But many a man had done that, without her reacting this weirdly. Anna was a true creature of the senses, using her female abilities to her best advantage almost on a daily basis - and she had succeeded very well with this approach in the past.

She wasn't a beautiful woman in the classic sense of the word. Her skin wasn't pale enough, her face was a little too round and she might just be a little too short for her beam. But that was compensated nicely by her shapely breasts and her big eyes. The eyes were blue or pale green, depending on the light at hand – and perhaps her mood. Her hair was long and curly and not exactly blond unless she had stayed too long in the sun. However, her main attractiveness lay not in her bodily features themselves, but in the way she used them.

The men she'd met had been too dazzled, enchanted, to even understand that she wanted something different from them than intimacy and sex – or they had not been able to resist her anyway. And being who she was, Anna usually felt attracted to her victims herself, making it much easier to be convincing.

Eric, however, was different. He had not been attracted to her from the beginning, rather the opposite. He had kept his distance, always being polite, but never crossing the line. When they finally did make love, it wasn't he who'd started it, and Anna had realized that Eric probably was the first man she'd met who really wanted her as a person, not only her body. And she had finally had to admit that she was in love with him as well.

She still did not think it would work in the long run. Eric af Klint was a nobleman and officer, and she was a poor mysterious girl who did not talk about her past, and who was deep into clandestine work, using her body as a tool. Eric knew this and had eventually convinced her to try being together anyway, at least over the winter. In the best of cases, this would be the beginning of something wonderful, but if it didn't work out, they still would have shared a few weeks of bliss.

Eric had gotten the fire going and was turning around, facing her. "I might not want the maid in here for a while just yet," he said, looking into Anna's eyes.

"Oh." Anna suddenly did not feel the cold any more as her body reacted to his words and the lust she saw in his eyes. She lifted the sheet and he slipped into the bed, his cold body pressing hard against the warmth of her. Anna sighed as he kissed her hungrily.

Two hours later they were having breakfast. The room was nice and warm and the coffee was fresh and hot. Eric af Klint looked out of the window. Snowflakes were falling lazily, some of them stuck to the glass of the window, slowly melting. He turned his head and saw Anna looking at him questioningly.

"What's on your mind?"

They had been in this house for many weeks now. Anna, Eric, the maid and a groom who tended the stable. It wasn't extraordinarily big, but it was an estate and it was Eric's. His parents were both dead, the father having been killed in the last war against Russia and his mother had died only a few years later. It was the perfect love nest, Anna thought. The estate lay to the west of Stockholm, surrounded by deep forests and farmland. In front of the house was a big lawn that slowly sloped down towards the water of lake Mälaren. In the summer, one could sail a boat from here right into the center of the capital. Now, of course, the boats were all hauled ashore as the ice on the lake became thicker for every day.

"Well," Eric said, looking at her, "I have been thinking for a while now – with the ice this thick..."

"Yes?" She looked at him curiously.

"Eh, well, we could take out the sleigh."

"Oh! Yes, darling, what a marvelous idea! Where are we going?"

"Well, in fact we might go to the city. If you don't mind, of course..." Looking a little worried.

"To Stockholm? Why should I mind, Eric?"

"Well, I thought, you might think it would break the spell, perhaps?"

Anna suddenly realized what he was thinking. They had been in this house together for weeks, never meeting any people except themselves. If they went to Stockholm, they would have to meet people, and now he was thinking that might shatter their blissful existence, pulling them apart. She put her hand firmly on Eric's. "You are so sweet, darling. Don't worry, I'd love to go to town. We could go to the theater, perhaps?"

Eric smiled. "Yes, we could. And we could meet Lieutenant Kuhlin and his wife, if you like."

"When are we leaving?"

Chapter 2 – Ice Piloting

During the night, the wind had eased a little and veered round to the Southwest. It was still blowing a good force six, normally warranting top gallants and reefed topsails, but being quite a little wary of the threat of ice, Captain Baker had ordered HMS Tartar to be under topsails only. Thus going slower, but steadily with the wind aft of the beam, the ship moved north towards the islands off the Swedish capital.

As a midshipman, Baker had been in a sloop of war on a mission to the Arctic sea. Chasing a French privateer, they had risked not only their lives, but their ship by cruising precariously near floating ice, growlers and even the occasional iceberg. Their prey, the privateer, had been a converted whaling ship, built much more sturdily and able to take the punishment from crushing ice – at least to a degree. They had taken her, but at a high cost indeed. Severely damaged by ice, with seams leaking and several fothering sails needed to keep her afloat, their ship had made it in the end, to the safe shelter of a British port, and a dry dock to take her in. But Baker had learned his lesson. Sailing into waters where there could be ice was not to be taken lightly at all.

When the ice forms in the Baltic, it starts from the North and from the land and slowly moves Southwards and out to sea. The Gulf of Bothnia, from its inner end towards the Åland islands usually freezes solid and so do the archipelagos along the east coast. However, it varies considerably how far the ice will extend out to the open waters of the Baltic proper. Some winters it covers most of it, some not. In any case, it usually covers the most in late January and early February.

When HMS Tartar closed the shore, there was still no sea ice that far South of Åland, although it had been reported that the inner archipelago was iced over considerably. Still, Baker hoped they would be able to bring the ship far enough into the channels between the islands to make a journey into the capital reasonably comfortable. Having discussed the matter with his Sailing Master, Mr. Pope, an experienced man in his late forties, Baker had decided on two favored anchorages. The first was only six miles from the capital itself at Baggensfjärden, just outside the small channel of Baggenstäket, where Swedish forces in a desperate effort had managed to stop the Russian assault in 1719. The channel itself would most certainly be blocked by ice, but outside was a fairly big stretch of water that might be open. To get to it, however, the frigate would have to maneuver through the narrows at Saltsjöbaden. This was difficult enough to do without the right wind, but if there was already ice, it would be impossible altogether.

The second alternative was Dalarö. About three times farther South, the trip into Stockholm would not be as comfortable, but on the other hand there was a fortress at Dalarö and a small settlement which hopefully would have a boarding house or tavern. There being a military presence also should imply that some means of communication would probably be in place. But you could never be sure with the Swedes, Captain Baker thought. After all they still didn't copper coat their ships against marine growth, rendering perfectly good vessels much slower than they could have been.

Baker donned his greatcoat and made his way up to the quarterdeck once again. It was still cold, but with the wind blowing less strongly, being outside didn't feel like imminent death any more. There were more men on deck forward now as well, mostly extra lookouts, but one group of men thrashed away at the lower shrouds with wooden clubs in order to remove the coating of ice that had formed on the tarred ropes. The ice did not only make it difficult for the crew to climb the rigging, if unattended it also could make the frigate top heavy. It was not uncommon for ships to capsize due to iced over rigging and sails.

Baker moved over to the binnacle and checked the compass.

"North-northeast as ordered, sir." Reeman, his first lieutenant, offered helpfully.

"The log?" captain Baker asked.

"Five knots, sir."

Baker grunted. Five knots was not fast for a frigate, but hitting solid ice at that speed could damage her nonetheless. Probably even sink her if the impact was in the right – or rather wrong – place. He considered ordering the topsails reefed to slow her down further, but decided against it. If they went too slowly they might not get to their destination before it was all iced over.

"Very well." Baker turned and started to stroll back to the warmth of his cabin when there was a shout from the foremast top.

"Deck there!"

"Go ahead!" Reeman acknowledged.

"Ice on the larboard bow!"

"How much of it?"

"Looks like a lot, sir!"

Captain Baker turned to his second in command.

"Go up there if you please, Mr. Reeman and take a glass with you."

"Aye aye, sir."

A few minutes later, the first lieutenant looked through his telescope at the distant white line to the northwest. It did not look as solid as he would have expected, like it could as easily have been a patch of fog or a low snowy skerry.

"What do you see?" The captain shouted impatiently.

"I'm not sure, it's still quite far away, sir. Could be fog perhaps?"

"I'm coming up."

Baker did not like going up into the rigging. Not that he was afraid of heights, he merely thought of it as a task not worthy a post captain. But this was important, none of the men up there had any experience of sailing in ice, and he had. So he bit his lip and climbed the cold tarry ropes. Once atop he took the telescope Reeman offered him and put it to his eye.

"That's ice, no doubt," he declared, moving the glass slowly to the right. "And there is an island. Hmm."

He put down the telescope and gave it back to the lieutenant.

"There is a stretch of open water between the ice and that island. We will alter course accordingly."

"Aye aye, sir". Both men descended to the deck carefully.

Two hours later, HMS Tartar was right in the middle of it. A vast expanse of ice stretched off her larboard side all the way to the distant coast. Farther to the North, a darker shadow loomed out of the whiteness, and on its seaward end showed something that looked like a small tower.

"That would be the Landsort lighthouse," the sailing master pointed out. All three officers stood on the quarterdeck, shivering.

"Landsort, eh?" Reeman said. "Sounds almost like Land's End. I wish it were..."

"Keep your mind on the task at hand, Mr. Reeman," Captain Baker snapped. This kind of piloting was not at all his kettle of fish.

"Sorry, sir. Um, sir, may I ask a question?"

Baker looked at him, smiling slightly now.

"Of course, Lieutenant."

"Well, I was thinking that, once we anchor, sir. If there will be ice all around us... Will we not be crushed?"

"A very good question, Mr. Reeman. However, from my experience in the Arctic, we will not. You see, it is not the ice itself that damages ships, it is the movement of it. When the ice moves with the ship trapped in it, the ice will press onto the hull and damage it eventually. But, if the ice is still and does not move, the ship sits in it like in a cradle and will be fine."

"I see." Reeman did not look entirely convinced.

"This is why it is so important that we anchor – or moor – in a place where the water is sheltered and the ice does not move. Fortunately, in between these islands, there is very little movement of the ice. It is much worse in the open waters of the Arctic, or, as we have done, when one moors directly to an iceberg just like it was a dock."

The lieutenant's eyes widened. "You can moor a ship directly to the ice?"

"Yes, sometimes there is no other alternative. The whalers do it all the time. They get their drinking water from the ice, do you see?"

Reeman swallowed. Baker looked at him, smiling broadly now.

"So you see, what we are up to is nothing in comparison. There will probably be lots of ships in the ice at Dalarö. You will see."

Chapter 3 – The Ride to Town

It was a glorious winter morning. Very cold indeed, but the sky was pale blue and the low sun was shining enough to make the whiteness of snow and ice glitter. Anna was slowly walking towards the edge of the frozen lake. The snow was almost knee deep, but there was a path that had been trampled down by the servants going for ice or water and of course by the horses and the sleigh that had been moved to the lake this morning.

She was dressed for travel. One of af Klint's old cloaks over her dress and an old fur cap that covered not only her head but her ears, as well as woolen mittens. Perhaps not the most endearing outfit she could imagine, but having several hours of travel in freezing temperatures ahead of her, she found comfort more important than looks.

Halfway down to the lake, Anna stopped and turned around, looking at the house where she had been living all these past weeks. She sighed. This was as close to paradise she would ever be. As close to happiness. Whatever was going to happen to her in the future, she would always remember this time of unconditional love and passion, these weeks of closeness with Eric. Of course, she was quite sure that this could not last. After all, there was still a war on, and Eric was an officer of the king. And she was a spy. When this winter was over, they would have to go back to their businesses, respectively, and that would surely tear them apart, would it not?

Anna continued towards the shore and the sleigh that waited there. It was old, an all wooden contraption with a single bench for passengers, a trunk at the back that could hold baggage or cargo. Two solemn looking horses waited patiently for their working day to begin. The groom was standing next to the sleigh, waiting.

"When did you use this thing last?" Anna asked, smiling.

"Oh, don't worry, miss, we use it all the time."

Anna raised an eyebrow. "So you say." She looked more closely at the passenger seat. It was an old wooden bench that would have made her think of sore bottoms if it hadn't been covered in an abundance of furs and sheepskins. She stepped closer and stroked a dark piece of fur that stood out from the others which were mostly light in color.

"This one is bear," the groom explained.

"Oh."

"Yes, it is very old. The rest are mostly sheep and reindeer. But it will keep you all warm during the ride, never you fear, miss".

Anna lifted the bear skin and lowered her face towards it, wanting to touch it with her face and smell it. Suddenly there was a hissing sound and she found herself staring into two golden eyes. She gasped. The cat had been lying curled up between the furs and was now glaring at her with its ears angled back, whiskers trembling defiantly. Anna held out her hand to the animal.

"Oh, sorry, I didn't mean to scare you... And such a pretty thing you are..."

The cat looked at her inquiringly, all gray, sprinkled with brown and black and a white neck, chest and front paws.

"I don't think we can take you with us, though," Anna said, stroking its head. The animal started to purr.

Half an hour later they were on their way. Anna and Eric were deeply buried under furs, their heads barely visible, if at all. They huddled together, his arm around her shoulders, her head resting against his neck. The sleigh was moving swiftly on the ice of the lake, in fact the ride was much more gentle than Anna remembered from her childhood. It was almost like sailing, but without the heeling and pitching.

"I remember it much more like riding a carriage," she said. "Much bumpier."

"Well, it can be bumpy as well," Eric explained. "It all depends on the surface, you see. On smooth ice like this it's very comfortable, but when you travel on land, on a snowy or icy road, it's much bumpier, worse than riding a carriage in fact, the sleigh not having any suspension at all."

"I see." She nuzzled her face deeper into the warmth of his neck. Nibbling softly at his earlobe. Whispering in his ear then. She felt his body tense with the sensation.

"This is like a fairy tale, darling."

Eric turned his head towards her face and kissed her. "Then you are my fairy."

Anna lifted her head and looked into his eyes. She started to say something, but kept her thought for herself. He might be more right than he knew. Because fairies could be quite evil at times.

They stopped for lunch a few miles outside the capital, not far from the royal palace at Drottningholm island. There was a small tavern near the bridge serving some hot soup as well as a tot of brandy.

"What are we going to do when we arrive at Stockholm?" Anna asked.

"Well, we will have to find a room at some boarding house, of course. Then I don't know. Would you like to call on the Kuhlins? Or check out the theaters?"

Anna looked at him, saying nothing.

"Or..." Eric started.

Anna smiled at him. "Or we do all this tomorrow."

Eric af Klint blushed.

Stockholm in the winter of 1809 wasn't a happy town. The atmosphere was subdued by sickness and disease – thousands of soldiers and sailors too weak to be moved elsewhere had to be accommodated in the capital. The hospitals, or what went under that name, were overcrowded and chances for survival were greater outside of them anyway. So instead ordinary people had to take in the survivors of the war, feed them and treat them in whatever way they could. In return, many got infected themselves.

But it wasn't only the health problems that marked the Swedish capital. The war still wasn't over and rumors of the Russian army finally having marched over the frozen Baltic to the Åland islands, or even the mainland proper, were the predominant topic for discussion. There was supposed to be an army on Åland still which could, perhaps, stop the enemy. If not, likely nothing could save the capital itself.

And then there was the question of the king. An increasing number of people found him a liability, a threat perhaps to the very existence of the nation. It wasn't just that he was losing the war, which was bad enough of course, but he did not even see it as a problem. In his mind, the war could still be won, Sweden could still play an important role in the destruction of Napoleon and all his allies. Which, as everyone except the king did know, wasn't only impossible but could not lead to anything less than utter disaster.

During the previous summer campaigns in Finland, the strength of the Swedish army had already been severely hampered by too many officers not being as loyal to the king as should be expected. The mighty fortress at Svensksund had been lost, not to Russian guns, but to the wavering morale of the Swedish officers that should – and could – have held it. With it, the major part of the inshore fleet's gunboats had been turned over to the enemy and then used against the remaining Swedish forces.

There were other examples. Examples of battles lost, or not even fought by officers who did not believe the king's words of great landing operations and counter-offensives from the North. Officers who silently had accepted that Finland was lost and that this wasn't necessarily a bad thing. Because the fact was that Sweden was broke. The war did cost far more than people's lives – it swallowed big amounts of money – money which the king did not have. Sure, there were British subsidies, but they weren't nearly enough. Now, the king had decided to blackmail the British for more money. If they wouldn't increase their payments, the king would deny his only remaining ally trade to the Western ports.

They found two rooms at Beckens inn near the Northern town limits. It had to be two rooms because they were not married and af Klint was, after all, a nobleman. Fortunately there was a convenient door between their rooms, enabling them to efficiently keep their privacy up and their clothes off.

"Look here, my dear," said af Klint, standing behind Anna at the window, his arms around her waist. "This is the very road the king's sleigh comes past almost every day on its way from the castle to the new palace at Haga."

"Really?" Anna leaned back into him and turned her face towards him. "Does he keep to a schedule? I mean, does everybody know when he passes through?"

Eric af Klint looked into her eyes and lifted an eyebrow.

"You are not thinking up some mischief now, are you, my little spy?"

She smiled at him. "On the contrary, you know I am loyal to the king. But it is always good to know any weakness an enemy might exploit."

"Indeed."

Eric took a firmer grip around her waist and pulled her closer to him as their lips met in a kiss.

Chapter 4 – The Embassy

"Now, Ambassador Merry, sir, would you pray care to tell me why I am here with a complete ship's crew freezing to death in the ice?" Captain Baker frowned at the British ambassador. He was in a bad mood altogether, having traveled all the way from Dalarö on horseback, in a blizzard, almost getting lost in the woods several times.

"I am truly sorry, dear captain," the ambassador replied calmly. "I know it takes some getting used to this climate during the winter. If one ever does...get used to it that is..." He hesitated for a moment.

"Still, I am glad you are here. Even though it had been better if you had been able to put your ship a little closer."

Baker started to become impatient. "We tried, sir, indeed we did. But the ice did not let us through at all."

It had been his first lieutenant, Reeman, who had taken the cutter on a reconnaissance trip from Dalarö only days before. They had pulled mostly, despite the wind being quite co-operative for sailing, because the men were so cold Reeman had decided to put them to work physically in order to keep them warm. They had pulled all the way to Älgö and the narrows before Baggensfjärden. There they had been thoroughly stopped by the ice. The narrows were completely blocked for at least half a mile and Reeman had been forced to return to Dalarö as quickly as he could or his cutter might have been frozen in as well.

"I see," the ambassador continued. "Now, captain, if you would like to take a seat and perhaps a glass of port, I will tell you about the... Situation here."

"Very well," Baker agreed. He placed himself close to the fire that was roaring in the fireplace, received his wine and looked at Merry questioningly.

"Well," the ambassador began. "As you know, of course, Britain and Sweden have been allies during this past year's war. Your ship is proof of it enough, together with the rest of your admiral's squadron. However, we did not only support the Swedish monarch with ships. In fact, most of the support has been funds, money. 1.2 million of their currency in fact."

Baker widened his eyes.

"Yes. But now, do you see, their king is broke. He cannot really afford to continue the war. He will never be able to relieve Finland, whatever he might say in public. Fact is, dear captain, he might not even be able to keep the Russians out of Sweden proper."

"Can we give him more money?" Baker asked.

"No. We are offering him the same amount as last year, but not one more penny."

"Why not? Surely, every ally against Bonaparte should be worth a lot."

"Well, two reasons. First, our government does not like to be blackmailed. The Swedes are threatening to close their western ports to our trade, do you see?"

"Oh."

"Second, we are not even sure this king of theirs will last the winter..."

Baker gasped. "What?"

"There are indications of revolution, dear captain."

"Like in France?"

"No, no, nothing of the kind, thank God. It is the nobility and military officers which might throw over this king."

"I see. But, sir, what is my role in all this? I cannot move my ship to fight until the ice goes away..."

The ambassador lifted his glass and took a slow sip at his port. Then he looked the captain straight into his eyes.

"You are to do nothing at all."

"But, sir...?"

"I will explain it to you in a minute, captain. Do you care for another glass of port?"

Captain Baker left the embassy none the wiser. He still did not know why his ship was here and what he was supposed to do. A frigate with a crew of 200 men isn't a great show of force and less so if she is frozen immovably in the ice, several miles from the capital where, or so Baker thought, the action was supposed to be. If there was to be any action at all.

The ambassador had pointed out that the British government had no intention to openly interfere in case there was a revolution. However, no matter how crazy he might be, the king, Gustavus IV Adolphus, was the legally reigning monarch in Sweden and an ally.

"So are we to give him refuge if there is a revolution? Is that why I am here?" Baker had asked.

"Perhaps, dear captain, perhaps," the ambassador had answered, and that had been as specific as it had gotten.

Facing the question whether to ride back to his ship at once or stay in the capital for another day, Baker decided to stay. After all, his ship wasn't going anywhere and it had been an awfully long time since he had been to a theater. But first of all he would find himself a good meal and a warm bed.

Chapter 5 – At the Theater

The next morning dawned cold and gray, promising more snow to come. Miss Anna and Eric af Klint took their sleigh to Södermalm in order to visit Johan and Charlotte Kuhlin. Kuhlin had been the commander of a squadron of gunboats the previous summer and af Klint had been his gunnery officer. During some dangerous endeavors they had become not only brothers in arms but friends, and when they parted company after the boat's return to the capital, af Klint had promised to keep in touch.

The Kuhlins lived in a small house on the heights of Södermalm, overlooking the main harbor of Stockholm and the navy yard where the gunboats and galleys of the inshore fleet were now stored and repaired, as well as new ones built. To get there, the sleigh could either take the way through the city center, over a bridge, past the big royal palace and the old town on its own little island, then over another bridge and up the steep slope to Södermalm. Of course, at this time of the year there was another alternative. If they dared, they could take the sleigh right out on the ice and go directly to their destination, not caring about bridges or roads.

Had he been alone, af Klint probably would have

done so, and perhaps the same would have applied to Miss Anna, who, after all, was an exceptionally daring young lady. But now, being together, in love, and in no hurry, they took the long way around. This also meant they got a good view of the royal palace and the fluttering activity in the most busy parts of the town. It being winter and bitterly cold did not lessen the activity at all. This was Sweden, and the people living here were used to cold winters and went about their business as usual.

Arriving at last, they got out of the sleigh and permitted the groom to take it to a nearby tavern, there to wait for their return. Eric af Klint knocked on the door and they were admitted by a maid who ushered them into a small parlor. Shortly after, Charlotte Kuhlin entered, a big smile on her face.

"Anna, Eric, oh, it's so good to see you!" she cried. "I had no idea you were in town."

"We just arrived yesterday," af Klint explained. "And may I say you look very well."

"Don't flatter me, Eric. I am glad however, that we had the fortune to escape the illness that seems to have affected so many people here. The hospitals are still crowded with the sick and many a poor family has been forced to make room for them in their homes. But let's not talk about these dreadful things. How are you Anna, you look like the weeks in the country did you very good indeed."

Anna blushed. "Oh, yes it was wonderful. So peaceful and quiet…"

"But now we thought we should meet some people after all," Eric continued. "And perhaps go to the theater."

"What a marvelous idea," Charlotte exclaimed. "I haven't been to a play for months. Perhaps we might all go together?"

"That was what we were hoping for," Anna said. "But, dear, where is your husband? He is not indisposed I trust?"

"Oh, no. He is at the navy yard, doing something naval, you know." Charlotte laughed. "He is a commander now, having gotten his promotion at last."

"Good for him," af Klint said, "and he might just be rid of those dreadful gunboats now. As a commander they will surely give him a bigger vessel next summer."

"He does very much hope so," Charlotte answered. "I guess that's why he is keeping himself available at the yard so much. Now, I am forgetting myself! Would you not want a cup of coffee?"

Coffee was served by the maid and the conversation turned towards plans for the evening once more. Charlotte produced a printed newspaper in which there were advertisements of the several theaters the capital had to offer. Stockholm wasn't a big city compared to London, Paris or Berlin, but thanks to the previous king, Gustavus III, there were more cultural establishments than normally would have been expected. Gustavus was known as "the theater king" and had been very fond of all things cultural. He even died after having been shot by an assassin while attending the opera. Of course he had also started the last war against Russia, but that was not really unusual for a Swedish king – rather something that should be expected.

Finally the decision was made to attend a popular English play at the new theater at Makalös, an old palace converted into a theater by Gustavus, of course. Eric af Klint had never been there, but Charlotte had and liked it very much indeed.

"It is a very pretty little theater," she said. "Quite unrivaled actually".

"You are so witty, my dear," a voice suddenly could be heard from the hallway.

"Johan, look who is here!"

With the commander finally at home and all formalities concluded, it was soon time for dinner.

Captain Baker ate his dinner alone at the fashionable inn overlooking the old town and the harbor. The food was quite good, he thought, considering how Sweden wasn't a very rich country and at war as well. But apparently there was no lack of provisions, if you could pay for it. Which he could. Having been a post captain for ten years he had made a small fortune of prize money, which he mostly kept tucked away in the bank. He was unmarried – feeling that he could not lay the hardships required of a wife to a navy captain in active service on any woman he loved. Not that there hadn't been a few who would have been prepared to endure the loneliness and fear for him never to return, but he was a man of principles – and then again he hadn't really been sure if it was him or his prize money that had attracted the prey, so to speak. Or if it was him who had been the prey.

He pushed the thought away and tried to concentrate on the port and cheese that concluded his meal. Suddenly his eyes caught a poster on the wall. It was for a theater play and although it was printed in Swedish he did recognize the name of the playwright. It was English.

"Oh, this is beautiful!" Anna gasped. And indeed it was. There was nothing of the glum feeling of war and doom in the theater during that evening. The play was no classic, but it was entertaining and made people laugh and yelp with surprise at the final scene before the intermission.

They had gotten seats on the balcony, providing them not only with a good view of the stage, but also a good peek at the people seated below. The theater was quite full and there was an even mixture of uniforms and civilian clothes. The ladies wore their finest dresses, many of them for the first time in months, just like Anna. In fact, the dress had been chosen by Eric especially for this event. It was fashionable, low cut in front and emphasizing her impressive cleavage. Charlotte wore a slightly less intriguing gown, but becoming her very well and stating her position as an officer's wife. Johan Kuhlin and af Klint wore their best uniforms, glittering away in the reflection of the hundreds of candles lining the walls.

Eric af Klint rose. "Shall I get you something to drink? I think we will have at least a quarter of an hour."

Anna put her hand on his arm. "I think I'd like to take a stroll. Have a peek at people?" She smiled, looking at Charlotte. "What do you think, dear?"

"I would very much like it. Let's all go," Charlotte suggested.

Having descended down the stairs to the great hall where waiters scurried around with trays, offering wine and brandy, they stopped and looked around, soaking up the atmosphere and reveling in the beauty and gaiety of the evening. Suddenly, Kuhlin gasped. "I cannot believe this! What on earth is he doing here?"

"Who?" Eric af Klint and Anna asked simultaneously.

"The gentleman over there, he is a British captain. I met him at sea last summer."

Eric af Klint remembered. "The frigate we met just before we took the Russian brig?"

"The very one. I have to go and talk to him." Kuhlin took his wife's arm and started to walk, Anna and Eric following in his wake.

"Captain Baker, sir!" Kuhlin cried.

"Ah, lieutenant, I am sorry to say, I do not recall your name..."

"Kuhlin, sir. And it's commander now."

"Ah, right, congratulations."

"Thank you, sir. May I introduce my wife, Charlotte. And this is Lieutenant Eric af Klint, my artillery officer...or so he used to be. And Miss Anna Wetterstrand."

"I am enchanted, madam, miss. Lieutenant." Baker's eyes returned to Anna. "Um, yes, very enchanted indeed."

Eric af Klint started to say something, but Anna squeezed his arm and smiled at the captain. "So what are you doing here in the middle of the winter? You are not trapped in the ice with your ship, are you?"

The captain looked at her questioningly. Then he returned her smile. "But yes, exactly so, miss. My ship is in the ice, at Dalarö and cannot move at all. I am positively trapped here."

"Oh." Anna's eyes widened. "Won't your men all freeze to death?"

"Not at all, miss, not at all. There is a fire in the galley do you see and we have pots of glowing coal. No there is a much higher risk of the ship catching fire than the men freezing to death, I think."

"You are almost being funny, captain." Anna winked at him.

"Sir," Kuhlin interrupted. "If you do not have to return to your ship immediately I would be honored if you would join us for dinner some time?"

Baker considered this. "I might stay here a few more days. I would be glad to accept your invitation, commander."

The bell rung then, calling them back to their seats.

Chapter 6 – Plans and Plots

The two men were already halfway through their dinner when the third one finally arrived. They sat at a window table in the dining room of Beckens inn, the very same where Miss Anna and Eric af Klint had taken their lodgings the day before. Both men had the stiff appearances of officers, although they wore civilian clothes on this occasion. They were young, in their twenties, and had not yet climbed very high in rank. The first, whose name was Dillquist, was an army ensign and had arrived recently from the front on Åland, carrying dispatches. His friend was a sub-lieutenant with the Royal guards regiment and his name was Winther.

Both men were nervous. When the third man arrived, they waved him towards their table and looked at him apprehensively. He was older than they were and looked a trifle shabby in his old thick woolen coat and tricorne hat. He called himself Gray, but they were certain this wasn't his real name. He probably just got inspired by his coat. Now he took off his hat and sat down at their table.

"Do I get something to drink here, pray?" He said.

Dillquist smiled warily. "Of course." He beckoned the waiter who came with another mug of beer. Gray took a sip and sighed. "Well, I don't think he'll do it."

"Why?" Winther asked.

"He thinks it's too dangerous."

"But it isn't dangerous at all! We have been watching the road for weeks, and there are almost never more than two or three servants and the groom. No escort, nothing."

"It's not that," Gray replied. "I agree, capturing him would be easy and so does he. The concern is what's to happen afterward."

"Most of the troops will do nothing." Dillquist was certain.

"Perhaps. But there needs to be someone in charge. A council of men or one important man. Someone."

"And why can't he be this man?" Winther frowned.

"He thinks he isn't high ranking enough. There needs to be order, do you see. And order cannot be kept by a council of low ranking officers, lieutenants or even captains."

"But he isn't low ranking."

"No. But he isn't famous or trusted enough. We need someone who has the support of most of the troops and the people. Someone like general Döbeln."

Winther gasped. "But Döbeln is loyal."

"Yes, unfortunately he is."

They were silent for a moment. Then Dillquist leaned forward and almost whispered. "What if we do it by ourselves. Today?"

Gray looked at him seriously. "Then you will get yourselves hanged. And start a civil war in the process."

"Ah, Captain Baker, good day to you, sir," Ambassador Merry said. "So good of you to come so quickly."

"Of course, sir." Baker replied awkwardly. He wasn't quite sure if the ambassador had objections to him still being in the city. Perhaps he should have gone back to his ship directly. But how was he supposed to gather information if he had to stay on his frigate, miles away from the capital?

The ambassador opened his desk and produced a written note. He read it through, like it was the first time he saw it. Which couldn't be true. He is groping for time, Baker thought.

Finally the ambassador coughed. "Well, captain, I am glad you are still here."

Baker relaxed as Merry continued. "Yes. Now I do not need to send a messenger out to that wilderness where your ship is."

"Bad news, sir?" Baker started to become

impatient.

"Indeed. Well. The Swedish king has decided to seize all English ships in harbors on his west coast."

Baker gasped. "But...?"

"There still being no ice yet, do you see. Unlike here, where you have been seized by the forces of nature, so to speak." He made a chuckling sound.

"But why?"

"As to be used in negotiation, of course. He wants more subsidies."

"Ah yes, you mentioned something of the sort." Baker remembered his last visit at the embassy. There had been talk of closing the ports. But seizing British ships?

"But isn't that an act of war? Seizing our ships?"

The ambassador looked at him gravely. "Technically yes."

"And what are we going to do about it?"

The ambassador frowned. "Nothing."

"Nothing?" Baker started to get angry. "But those are British ships!"

"Yes, yes. But they will not sail until spring anyway. And by then..."

Baker widened his eyes.

"By then there will be another king?"

Merry smiled. "I do believe so."

"What do you want me to do, sir?"

The sleigh was gliding effortlessly over the brownish white surface of the road. Snow, days old and packed by sleighs, carriages, feet and hooves, turned into sleet and then into ice by the cold of the next night, made for a good ride. Anna cuddled closely to af Klint under the warm furs. His right arm was around her waist, hugging her close into the warmth of his body. Only their faces were peering out of the furs into the dark of the evening. They had dropped off the Kuhlins at their home and were now on their way towards their lodgings.

Eric af Klint turned his face towards hers and looked into her glittering eyes. She smiled at him in return. "Thank you for taking me here, darling," she whispered, her mouth close to his.

Eric kissed her softly, savoring the warm moistness of her lips. Anna moaned and opened her mouth to him and the kiss grew deeper, hotter, their mouths melting together. Anna's arms slid around him, dragging him down under the furs.

Suddenly the sleigh lurched violently. Anna gasped as their heads shot up out of the furs. Another sleigh had appeared out of the dark, almost colliding with theirs as it tore past and disappeared ahead.

"What was that?" Anna growled.

Eric looked at her face and started to laugh. "That, my dearest, was the king."

Anna's jaw dropped. "The king?"

"I believe so. He usually takes this route on his way to the palace at Haga where he lives."

"But doesn't he have an escort?"

"No, I don't think he ever has. Perhaps he thinks his sleigh is so fast, nobody could catch him."

"That's not funny Eric!" Anna's eyes were still wide in astonishment. "You know there are people who would want him dead."

"I know, darling."

"So shouldn't he have some protection?"

"Probably yes. But it is his decision. He is the king."

Anna frowned.

The two young officers were still sitting at their table when the king's sleigh sped past outside the window.

"There he is," Dillquist said, his voice low.

"Only he and the groom," Winther added.

Simultaneously they took another sip at their beers. A short while later, Anna and af Klint entered through the front door and strolled past them towards the stairs to their rooms on the first floor.

Chapter 7 – Suspicions

Captain Baker was freezing. About an hour after he started his journey back to Dalarö and his ship it had started to snow. Thick white snowflakes danced everywhere around him. In fact, everything was white, it felt like he was sailinged in dense fog. And it was so quiet. Aboard ship, there were always noises, even in a calm. And there were always people. But here was only cold white nothingness. Except for him and the horse he was riding. And some peculiar horse it was. Some Nordic breed, well accustomed to the cold weather, it was small, not much bigger than a pony. Trotting along well enough, it sometimes started to pace in a most uncommon way, making him almost seasick before he got the animal to walk decently again.

He smiled to himself at the thought of a Royal Navy captain being seasick on horseback. Then he became serious again, wondering how long he could go on like this. Could he even be sure he was on the right road? He couldn't see much more than fifty yards ahead in this snow and there might be any number of junctions he could have missed. Finally he saw a small cottage next to the road. Baker halted his horse and jumped into the snow and walked up to the door. He knocked.

The door was opened by a young woman in a simple dress. She did not speak any English and very little French, but she admitted him into the kitchen and beckoned him to sit at the fire.

"Thank you very much," Baker tried. But the girl only gave him a shy smile and disappeared through another door.

"Ah, now what business does an officer have out in this weather?" An older man entered through the same door the girl had vanished. He held out his hand. "And a foreign one as well."

"Ah, yes, Captain Baker of the British navy." Baker shook the man's hand.

"Are you a sailor yourself?"

The man nodded. "I used to be. But I am too old now. A bosun I was, on the Camilla."

"That's a frigate, isn't it?"

"Aye. And one of our best. Almost got to battle your ships in 1801 we did."

Baker smiled warily. "I heard about that. Off your west coast. Well we weren't allies then."

"Aye. Now, do you care for something hot to drink, sir?"

"Yes, thank you very much. I have to admit I am frozen quite solid."

The old man laughed. "My daughter will make us

some soup."

"Eric?" Anna lifted her face and looked at the man next to her in the bed. The small room was warm, with a fire blazing in the iron stove and they were naked. "Did you notice the two men sitting at the window table when we came in?"

"Hmm." Eric looked at her, raising an eyebrow. "What about them?"

"They were here yesterday as well."

"So?"

"And I think I have seen one of them before. The younger one? He wore a uniform then, just before we left Åland last autumn."

Eric considered this. "So he is on leave, perhaps?"

Anna frowned. "The army isn't on leave. They aren't hindered by the ice like your boats."

"Yes, but he might be here temporarily, perhaps carrying dispatches."

"Then he should be wearing his uniform, should he not? And he shouldn't sit here and watch the king's sleigh pass every night."

Eric smiled. He put his right arm around her and his hand started to trace the delicate lines of her body, from the neck downwards. He stopped in the small of her back.

"You know what I think?" He said softly.

Anna raised an eyebrow questioningly.

"I think, my little spy is coming awake again."

Anna frowned at him and opened her mouth to speak, but he gave her no chance. He slid his other arm under her waist and, tightening his grip, lifted her on top of him. Anna yelped in surprise as she felt him ready and eager between her thighs. Propped up on her arms on either side of his body she looked into his eyes and the raw passion she saw there made her almost blush.

She lowered her face and kissed him then, tasting his desire for her. Her breasts were just touching his chest and the sensation made her shiver. Pulling away from his mouth at last, she pushed her body lower towards him. His hands were on her buttocks now, guiding her onto him as he entered her slowly. Anna moaned and pressed herself against his body as hard as she could, letting him fill her completely.

Captain Baker stayed at the cottage over night, sleeping on a narrow bench in the kitchen. But it was warm and his belly was full. It had been interesting to chat with the old bosun as well. Baker learned a few things about the Swedish frigates and how they were handled. He was astonished that their hulls still were not copper coated against the ship worm and marine growth. But the bosun had told him that the water in the Baltic did not hold the worm due to its low salinity.

"Still, there must be other growth that slows the ships down?"

"Aye, 'tis true. But I reckon it's a question of money in the end."

To that, the captain could say nothing. It was the same in his navy after all. Even if the copper coating was standard now, there still were lots of other things to save money on. Like paint, or powder and shot.

While they had been talking, the daughter had been sitting quietly, repairing a piece of clothing. She was a pretty enough girl, Baker had thought and something must have shown in his eyes, because the bosun had told him that she was married then.

"Married to a soldier, she is. But if he is still alive, we do not know..."

The next morning the snowing had stopped and Baker was able to resume his journey. It was still cold, almost colder still than the day before, but at least the sun was shining and the landscape was all aglitter with reflections from the snow. Baker literally had to squint in order not to be blinded.

However, the road lay clear ahead and he made it to Dalarö by lunchtime. Leaving his horse at the small tavern in the village, he walked towards the docks and saw his ship once again. The ice was thick around the frigate now, in fact thick enough for it to bear both man and horse. There were other ships in the anchorage, frozen in as well. Most of them were merchant ships, brigs and flat bottomed things with a cutter rig, designed to carry a huge deck cargo of wood.

Baker shuffled carefully towards his ship. This felt wrong, you weren't supposed to walk on your own feet towards a frigate at anchor. But walk he did and when he was a few yards away, a marine sentry challenged him formally, even though he could clearly see who he was.

"Tartar!" He answered equally formally, stating his position as the ship's commanding officer. He then walked towards the side of the ship and climbed aboard her like he had been carried there in his gig. The bosun's pipe shrilled.

On deck, he was greeted by his first lieutenant.

"Welcome back, sir!"

"Thank you, Reeman. Please pass the word for all officers, I'd like them in my cabin at once."

"Aye, aye, sir."

"Oh, and tell the galley to bring us something hot. I don't care what it is, as long as it warms me up."

Ten minutes later, his officers had gathered in the frigate's great cabin. A brazier with glowing coal was holding the worst of the cold at bay, but still the men were all wearing their greatcoats.

"Well, gentlemen," the captain said. "I am sure you are very eager to hear the latest news."

The men nodded.

"It is not very good at all. The news." Captain Baker coughed. "The Swedish king has apparently decided to seize all British shipping on his west coast."

There was a nervous shuffle among his officers.

"Yes. Now, this does only apply to merchant ships at the moment and not at all on this coast. Nonetheless we will make ready our guns and double our marines' guards."

"Shall we clear for action?" Reeman asked.

"No. I don't think that is necessary at the moment."

"Aye aye, sir".

"Now, also be aware that there are many rumors about revolution, and it might very well be so that the king is not to be king for very much longer."

More shuffling. Then Reeman spoke. "I am sorry, sir, but I still do not understand what is to be our part in all this."

Captain Baker grunted. "Neither do I, Mr.

Reeman. But I am confident it will all come to light, eventually. In the meantime, gentlemen, I want you to ponder about another little problem. As you know the sea is all frozen toward the capital. But it is only a few miles to open water the other way. So would there be a way to get out – if it should occur that we must?"

He looked around at his officer's faces but saw nothing but incomprehension.

Lieutenant Kuhlin was sitting as his desk when his wife brought him the note.

"It looks like there will be no dinner with that English captain of yours," she said, handing him the single sheet of paper.

"Oh." Kuhlin read it. "Well, he had to go back to his ship. Naturally enough I suppose. Still I wonder why the hurry. After all his frigate is frozen in and cannot move for weeks... Or months."

Charlotte looked at him questioningly. "Johan?"

"Yes darling?"

"Why are you so interested in this British captain?"

Kuhlin frowned. "Well, to be frank, I think he owes me money."

Charlotte's eyes widened. "Owes you money?"

"Well, not he personally, I suppose. But, do you

see, last summer we helped him capture this Russian brig, hiding in between the islands, in waters too shallow for his ship to pursue. And I never got any prize money."

Chapter 8 – Discoveries

The two men were all soaked with perspiration in the hot, steamy air of the sauna. They were sitting on the top bench of three, nearest the roof and thus the hottest air, totally naked, except for a thin cloth around their waists. The air was heavy and moist with steam – one of the girls had just thrown a bucket of water on the hot stones atop the iron wood stove. She wore only a thin linen gown which clung to her body like a second skin, wet as it was.

Ensign Dillquist looked at the girl lazily, wondering how she could work all day long in this heat. But probably they got used to it, he thought. As well as to the naked men and women who visited this place.

Public bathing houses, saunas, had been in existence in the Swedish capital for at least a hundred years. They had once started as a place for ordinary people to clean themselves up and do their laundry as there weren't too many homes that had the necessary facilities for it. But just like the ancient Roman baths they had become much more than that. Now they were places where people could meet for a chat while they subjected their bodies to the sensual delights of being thoroughly warm despite freezing outside temperatures and purge their pores of dirt, sweat and whatever they might hold. In fact, a sauna bath was at least as health-restoring as a good session of bloodletting.

Of course, the best sauna is the private one, a small hut with just one or two wooden benches and an iron stove, near a lake or beach, with a jetty to deep enough water for a plunge. A plunge that, during the winter, could be taken right into the ice cold water in a hole sawn into the ice.

But here, in the city, such a thing was not to be had. Instead the public bathing house, located in the basement of an old stone building in the southern part of the town, featured a much larger room, a much larger stove and two big wooden tubs, filled with water. One of those was currently occupied by a middle-aged woman. Despite her being completely immersed in the water, enough of her pale flesh was visible to attract Dillquist's attention. He was, however, not aroused in the least, his interest merely being a lazy kind of curiosity. After all, there was not a man in the world, who would not look at any naked female, if only for a short second.

Apart from the woman in the tub, there was another customer. An old man was sitting on the lowest bench, farthest away from the stove. The second of the two girls who worked the place was flogging him lightly with a birch twig complete with leafs and everything to increase his blood circulation and purge his pores more efficiently. The sauna girls were famous for having no shame at all, working the whole day amongst naked people, rubbing them with sponges and showering them with buckets of water. However, they were not whores and any attempt to take advantage of them would have been unthinkable. At least while they were working, thought Dillquist. Although the little one who just entered with another bucket of water to be thrown on the stones was exceptionally exquisite indeed.

"Don't even think of it," the man next to him said. It was, of course, sub-lieutenant Winther.

Dillquist sighed. "You know, it must have been months ago I even saw a girl with so few clothes on. Let alone touched her."

"There will be plenty of time for distractions like this later," Winther replied. "But now we have more important tasks at hand."

Dillquist struggled to keep his eyes off the girl. "I know. But I am getting a little too hot here."

He raised his hand and made a sign to the girl. "A bucket of water, please."

She smiled at him. "Coming right up, sir."

Winther frowned. "Now, tell me. What do you think General Döbeln would do, if our plan came through?"

"I don't think he would do a thing. He is indeed loyal to the king, that's for sure. But he has his hands full with the Russians. They are to march over the ice and attack him any day now. They might have done it already for all I know, what with the news traveling so slowly."

The girl came back in then and climbed up to them. She crouched next to him and started to slowly pour water over his body from the bucket she had been carrying. Dillquist sighed and looked at her. "Thank you."

She smiled, still pouring water. Dillquist felt the warmth of her body next to him, smelled her fresh sweat through the moist linen gown. It wasn't an unpleasant smell, not at all like the stale old sweat of an army tent at night, but a sweet, almost promising scent. Like the smell of a girl when you have sex with her, Dillquist thought. He was suddenly aware that his thoughts were showing under the thin cloth that covered his groin. He turned back to Winther abruptly.

"So don't worry about Döbeln," he continued. "Instead, we should be thinking about what our friend Gray is worrying about."

"Ah," Winther said. "Gray is just a scared old man."

"No. I think he has a point. You can't just start a revolution. You need to have a plan as for who is to be in charge afterward."

"Do you want me to fetch another bucket?" the girl asked, smiling.

General Döbeln did indeed have other things to worry about. He was, of course, aware there were plans for a coup d'état in the capital. However, he was confident that nothing would come of it in the end. After all, there had been rumors for months but nothing had happened. The police were also aware of the problem and would certainly keep their eyes open. So Döbeln concentrated on defending the Åland islands. There had already been skirmishes with Russian cavalry, cossacks, who had been probing the Swedish defenses.

And it was March now. The ice would not be safe for more than another month at most and surely not even the Russians would advance over so late that they couldn't be sure they could ever get back. They were confident of winning this war, and Döbeln had to admit that they would, lest there was any chance of a diplomatic solution. A solution which certainly would entail the loss of Finland and probably even of the Åland islands. Still, he would make his stand as he was ordered to do.

However, Döbeln wasn't the only general in the Swedish army. And others weren't as loyal to the king as he was. One of them was Adlersparre, and on March 6th his army had occupied the city of Karlstad deep in the forests to the West. From there, he would march towards the capital, in order to overthrow the king by force, thus bringing Sweden to the brink of civil war.

Commander Kuhlin was having coffee with his wife when there was a knock at the door. The maid put down her tray and went to answer it. When she reappeared with the visitor in tow, Kuhlin rose with a broad smile. "Bosun Tapper! Pray come in. How are you doing?"

"Well, just fine, sir. Thank you, sir."

Tapper, who had been bosun on Kuhlin's boat during the last summer's campaign, was placed at the table and served a steaming cup of coffee. "You want something strong in that?" Kuhlin asked.

Tapper nodded, grinning. Kuhlin poured a reasonable amount of vodka into the coffee.

"You like it as they say in the North, don't you? Enough coffee to make the bottom of the cup disappear, and then as much vodka as it takes to be able to see it again?"

"Aye." Tapper lifted the cup and took a sip. Then

he sighed.

Kuhlin watched him. "Is everything alright, Tapper?"

The bosun looked down into his coffee for a while. Then he coughed and started to speak. "Well, sir, to be frank, I don't know. You see, I've been seeing this girl lately..."

Charlotte Kuhlin widened her eyes. "Oh! So good for you." She smiled at him. The bosun actually blushed under his beard. "Eh...Well, madam..."

"Go on, Tapper," Commander Kuhlin encouraged.

"Well, sir, do you see, she works at this bathing house... And...."

Kuhlin laughed. "You got yourself a sauna girl?"

Tapper blushed deeper.

"Sorry, bosun, I couldn't resist." He chuckled.

"They are not whores, Johan," Charlotte said, her eyes narrowed.

"I know, dear, I'm sorry. I am glad for you, Tapper. Please continue."

The bosun took a deep gulp of coffee. "Eh, yes. Well, sir, she works at this sauna, alright. And yesterday she told me of those men who she had heard talking and...."

"Ah, she was eavesdropping?" Kuhlin couldn't resist. "Her name is not possibly Anna, is it?" He grinned.

Tapper looked dumb founded. "No, it's Karin. Why?"

Charlotte put her hand on his arm. "Don't pay attention to him, bosun. He is pulling your leg. He thinks you got yourself a spy of your own – just like our dear gunner."

"But no, sir, madam, she isn't like that at all. Really. She is the sweetest girl I've ever met. And so clean and..."

Kuhlin coughed. "Yes, Tapper. I'm sorry, I didn't mean to offend you...."

"...or her." his wife added.

"Yes, dear. So please do continue. Who were those men and what were they talking about?"

Tapper lifted his cup but found it empty. Charlotte beckoned the maid to fill it and Kuhlin added the same amount of vodka as before. Another gulp and Tapper was ready to continue.

"Well, they were talking about revolution, sir."

Kuhlin lifted an eyebrow. "A lot of people are doing that these days, Tapper."

"I know, sir. But they were talking about... Well, matters of fact. You see, they knew things. About Döbeln and the Åland defenses..."

"So they are probably officers..."

"...And they had been checking on the king and noting times and routes... When he rides his sleigh between the palace and Haga."

Kuhlin scowled and his wife widened her eyes. "That might be serious enough?" she said.

Commander Kuhlin nodded. "You should probably talk to the police about this," he proposed.

The bosun frowned. "No, I won't talk to no police. They'd just pin it on us, or ask her improper questions, or..."

Kuhlin could understand him. The police didn't have the best of reputations. But whom could he talk to instead, when one couldn't even know for sure which officers were still loyal to the king? He sighed.

"Could he talk to Anna?" Charlotte suggested.

Kuhlin thought about that. In fact, he didn't even know to whom Anna Wetterstrand answered. She had been a spy during the last summer's campaign in the Finnish archipelago, and then he had received his orders concerning her from the commodore of the squadron. She had been involved in the discovery and finally the death of another spy, or traitor then, and it was clear that she was loyal to the king. But Kuhlin did not know who her superiors were, what rank she had – if there was such a thing as rank in the clandestine trade at all – and if she still was on their payroll. After all, she and af Klint had been tucked away in that estate of his for weeks. But on the other hand – it surely couldn't hurt to ask her advice.

"Yes," he said, making up his mind. "That would probably be best. I will send her a note."

"I could go there myself, if you like? Don't want to trouble you, sir," Tapper offered.

"No trouble, bosun. You stay right here and have another tot."

Chapter 9 – Expertise

Lieutenant Reeman entered the great cabin aboard HMS Tartar in order to see the captain. Baker himself was sitting at his desk, writing in a notebook. He looked up at his second in command and smiled.

"Ah, you are back. Pray sit down Mr. Reeman."

The lieutenant sat, still shivering from the cold outside. "I can't believe this cold, sir. How could you ever survive in the Arctic? I hear it's much colder there still."

"Well," the captain said. "It is indeed colder there, but it does not feel so much colder in fact. I understand it has something to do with how much moisture the air holds. Moisture always makes the feeling worse. And in the Arctic, the air is very dry, while here it holds much more water."

Reeman nodded. "Ah, yes, it's the same with heat, isn't it? In the tropics the air feels much hotter than in Egypt, even though the temperature itself can be higher in the desert."

"Exactly, Mr. Reeman. Now what have you found out?"

"Um, yes. It is like you thought, sir. About two

nautical miles, perhaps a little more."

"And how thick is the ice?"

"Well, we drilled through it at several places and it is about a foot thick almost everywhere."

"And the surface?"

"Smooth, sir. Much smoother than I thought actually. There is snow on top of it of course."

"Very well," Baker said. This was very good indeed. He had sent Reeman and a small party of men to explore the ice between the frigate and the more open waters to the southwest. As he had suspected, the ice was only solid between the islands off Dalarö and in the narrow part of the sound between it and the bigger island of Ornö. Already at its southwestern tip the sound widened and there the water was almost open, except for a few floating floes.

And even better was that the ice was smooth and not very thick. Of course, a foot of ice was thick enough to ride a horse on, so it wouldn't be easy to force the frigate through it, but he had some notion of how it could be done. Perhaps.

Reeman looked at him questioningly. "May I ask what you are planning, sir?"

Baker smiled. "Of course, Mr. Reeman. Do you see, when I was on that sloop of war in the Arctic, we met a few whalers who told stories of how they escaped the ice in much more pressing situations than this. In the Arctic the ice is not only much thicker, it isn't as smooth either, what with currents and storms pressing floes on top of each other into near impenetrable ridges of ice. Mountains almost if you want."

Reeman's eyes widened. "So how did they do it?"

"There are basically two ways. You can saw yourself a canal right through the ice. But then you need special ice saws which we do not have."

"And the other way?"

"You blast your way through it."

Reeman startled. "You mean with gunpowder?"

"Exactly. Mr. Reeman. And of that, we have plenty, do we not?"

Reeman nodded.

"However," the captain continued. "As the ice here is much less thick, there might just be a third way…"

"And that would be, sir?"

Baker smiled mysteriously. "I'd rather think about it a little more first."

Anna arrived at the Kuhlins' house only one hour after they had sent the messenger. Of course, the message hadn't said anything about her needing to come right away, merely a notion about Tapper's predicament and if she might have any idea about how he could proceed with the matter. However, Anna being who she was, found her curiosity stirred to such a degree that she decided to go herself.

"I haven't been doing anything useful for all these weeks," she had said to Eric, who had flinched at her words like he had been hit. Anna had kissed him then, deeply, until she had felt him relax. "I did not mean it that way, darling," she had explained. "Of course being with you has been wonderful and I would not have wanted to do anything else."

He had smiled warily then, knowing what she would say.

"But I am not made for domestic bliss only, Eric. I need to feel more alive than that."

"Do I not make you feel alive?" He had asked.

She had sighed and held his face between her hands.

"Don't make this more difficult than it needs to be, darling. I love you more than anyone. But I cannot give up this other life of mine. I need to be myself."

Eric had sighed, too, then. "I know. I'm sorry. I just don't want to lose you."

"You will never lose me." She had kissed him again then. "I'll be back soon enough."

MISS ANNA'S FRIGATE

At the Kuhlins' house Anna was welcomed warmly and served coffee with a tot as well as Tapper's story.

"I want to meet your girlfriend, Tapper," she said finally. "I need her to describe these men in as much detail as possible."

"Do you think you might know who they are?" Charlotte asked.

"Perhaps. It's really quite far fetched, but I have observed two men at our inn lately who, well, let's say I think they behaved suspiciously."

Tapper coughed suddenly, looking embarrassed.

"What is it, bosun?" Anna asked.

"Eh, sorry, Miss. Do you want to meet her, like right now?"

"As soon as possible, I think."

Tapper blushed deeply under his beard.

"Out with it, Tapper!" Commander Kuhlin said. "Is there a problem? Don't you know where to find her or what?"

Tapper cleared his throat. "Of course I know where to find her, sir. It's just that..."

Anna laughed. "Oh, bosun, I see. She is at work, isn't she?"

Tapper nodded, looking at the floor.

"Perfect!" Anna exclaimed. "A visit to the sauna is just the right thing in this cold. Come on, Tapper!"

"Now, bosun, tell me, how did you meet this girl, what's her name?" Anna asked on the way to the bathing house.

"Karin." Tapper was still embarrassed by all of this and he nearly regretted having gone to Kuhlin with this matter. It was always like this in the navy – if you volunteered for anything at all, you could consider yourself lucky if you came out of it alive. However, in this special case it was not so much his life that was in danger but his sense of decency. Which perhaps was uncommonly well developed for a petty officer.

He looked at Anna and realized she was still waiting for an answer. "Eh, well I didn't meet her at the sauna if that's what you're thinking." He said at last.

Anna smiled at him. "I am not thinking anything at all. I am just curious."

Tapper took at deep breath. "She is a friend of a friend of mine's daughter."

"Ah." Anna said. "I see, there is nothing to be embarrassed about then, is there?"

"No."

"So why are you embarrassed?"

Tapper stopped walking and looked at her. "Look, miss. I am not embarrassed about her, or her working at the sauna. It's not that."

"So what is it then, bosun?"

"It's just that... Damn it. I haven't been that intimate with her yet! And now I am supposed to see her there like – you know what they are wearing. And then you..."

Anna tried not to laugh. "What about me?"

Tapper blushed. "Yeah, what are you going to wear?"

She was laughing now. "You are not supposed to wear anything in a sauna, Tapper."

Suddenly he laughed as well. "That's the problem."

"Don't worry, Tapper. You will be fine."

"I doubt it," he muttered but continued to walk.

When they arrived at the bathing house, Anna turned towards him. "You know, bosun, you don't have to go inside if you don't want to. I can do this alone perfectly well. I'll just ask for her and introduce myself."

Tapper hesitated. "No, miss. I am going in."

"You want to see her as well, don't you?" She smiled at him, her eyes glittering.

They paid their fee to an old woman sitting behind the door. Anna paid extra for some towels and then they entered. First they came to a room that contained wooden benches and shelves along the walls. Some of them held other customers' clothes, but most were empty. They hung their coats on wooden pegs under the shelves and then Anna started to take off her dress. Tapper turned to face the wall and fumbled with his breeches.

"Don't be shy, bosun," he heard her say with a chuckle. "You will see it later anyway."

Tapper turned then and saw her standing naked, smiling at him. Her breasts really are big, he thought, fighting down another blush. But he realized, almost with relief, that he could look at her like this without a problem. Probably because she wasn't the type of woman he liked best. While her face was more pretty than beautiful, her body was truly delightful – if you liked a woman with lots of curves, hills and ravines. She looked soft and something about her made him want to touch all that flesh. But then he thought about the thin, slender body of the girl who would be inside, his Karin, and that made him smile and hurry with the removal of his own clothes.

They entered the sauna proper. The hot humid air pushed against them heavily and made them gasp as they came through the door. Anna's eyes started to tear and she closed them to blink away the moisture. There were only two other customers in the room and they weren't those they were looking for. Two sauna girls were there as well.

Tapper saw Karin immediately. She was sitting on the lowest bench, a wooden bucket of water at her feet. She was very short and slender with a body almost like a boy's, except for her waist and hips and small perky breasts. Her face was round with pale blue, almost grayish eyes. Her hair was blond and thin and because it was wet it lay plastered against her cheeks and neck. She wore the usual thin linen dress which clung tightly to her body because of the moisture. To Tapper she looked positively lovely.

When she saw the new customers enter, she got up to greet them. Recognizing Tapper, she blushed deeply and gasped. "Oh."

It was then that Tapper realized what she must be thinking, seeing him enter with another woman. A naked woman. He suddenly felt completely at a loss. It was Anna who had to save him. She smiled at the young girl in front of her and said: "You must be Karin? Our bosun here has told me so much about you. Now I see why he likes you so much."

Karin blushed deeper but stood silent, clearly not knowing what to do with this situation.

"May we sit down with you?" Anna continued.

"I suppose so..." Karin looked at Tapper, who still stood like frozen. Anna followed the girl's gaze and put her hand on Tapper's arm. "Come on bosun, try to relax, will you."

Tapper moved slowly towards the bench, his eyes all on the sauna girl. "I'm sorry to burst in here like this," he finally managed to say.

Karin raised an eyebrow. "You were to see your commander, were you not?" She said sceptically.

"So he did, and the commander asked for my help," Anna explained.

Karin still looked unbelieving.

"You see," Tapper started, but then his voice faltered and he clutched at the towel he had placed in his lap so it would cover what was now apparently stirring after all. "God, you are so lovely!"

Karin, brightening, smiled at him. "It's just the heat, Carl, it's how I look at work..."

"But I mean it, dear, I wouldn't want you otherwise, ever!" He blushed. "I could stay here all day, just looking at you."

Karin laughed. "You know, I wouldn't mind it, actually, what with all the women you seem to know quite intimately..."

Anna chuckled. "Actually, Karin, seeing the way he looks at you, I think you could put him into a Botticelli painting and he would still only notice you."

"Botti..what?" Karin looked bewildered.

"Never mind, dear. My name is Anna by the way.

And the commander really asked me to help in this little matter of yours."

"But you are... Are you saying you are some sort of police?"

"No, not at all."

"She's a spy, Karin." Tapper said, keeping his voice low, although the room was big enough for them not to be overheard.

The girl looked at Anna. "Are you, really?"

"Well. Let's say I have been conducting a little cloak-and-dagger business before."

Karin widened her eyes. "I'd never known that there could be female spies!"

"You have no idea." Anna smiled at her.

"And is that how you met? You and the commander and Carl?" With the first shock having died down, the girl's curiosity had finally taken over.

"Yes," Tapper said. "She was, well, a passenger on our boat for a while last summer."

"So, please, Karin," said Anna finally. "Would you care to describe the two men you told the bosun about as thoroughly as you can?"

Chapter 10 – Complications

The king, of course, was continuously briefed about the unrest in his country. The problem only was that he did not care very much about it. Living quite in another reality altogether, one that was dominated by thoughts of him successfully battling the dominance of Bonaparte – as well as the design of new fancy uniforms and medals for his starving troops, he neither saw the danger closing in on him nor made any real plans to counteract it.

In fact, Gustavus Adolphus could not imagine his loyal subjects even thinking of such a thing as replacing him. Let alone his officers. Thus it wasn't until after the news of the military coup at Karlstad reached the capital that countermeasures started to be discussed.

First of all, the police were to seek out and question certain people who were thought to be capable of pulling off such a horrendous plot. There being quite a lot of possible suspects, this was, however, a strenuous task, and one that held very little hope of leading to any results before it would be too late.

So the king needed a second plan of action. He still did have loyal troops. Döbeln's coastal army for one thing, but the general was very much occupied with defending the Åland islands against the Russians. Other troops were further south, at Norrköping, a little less than 130 miles from the capital. With Karlstad being more than twice as far away, there was still time. Adlersparre's mutinous troops would need at least two weeks to march to Stockholm, probably longer in this weather.

However, there were lots of potential mutineers in the capital as well. And the king wasn't safe until he could be sure of the loyalty of all the officers in his vicinity. Thus, it was probably better for him to travel to Norrköping in person in order to make a stand there.

But could he just leave the capital without admitting defeat?

Anna Wetterstrand paced restlessly across the room while Eric af Klint sat on the bed watching her. He was not at all happy with this situation, but he knew he must hold his tongue or he would lose her. Knowing this did not make it any easier, though. It wasn't as much the thought of what she could be doing if she took up her clandestine activities again. Things like letting other men touch her. He sort of could accept that, or so he thought, as long as he knew that it was him she loved. No, it was the danger she was going to get herself into again. The possibility that she could be hurt, or die. And the fact that he could do absolutely nothing about it.

Anna stopped walking and looked at him. "Eric, darling, please stop frowning like that or you will get permanent wrinkles."

That made him laugh. "I'm sorry," he said.

Anna sat down next to him on the bed and took his hand in hers. "I know this isn't easy for you, Eric. But..."

"I know." Eric lifted her hand to his face and brushed it lightly with his lips. "I knew from the beginning that you would..." he hesitated. "...start spying again."

"It's what I can do to help in this war. To help the king."

"I know," Eric said again. "And I would not want you not to, really. Not for me... Or us."

"Eric, I understand if you..."

"No." Eric let go of her hand and cupped her face in his hands instead. "I love you, Anna. Whatever you do, I always will. You do what you need to do and I will be there for you. Now or later. Whenever you need me."

He saw her eyes fill with moisture.

"I love you, too, Eric. And soon this war will be over." Her voice was throaty with emotion.

Eric kissed her then, softly first, but when he felt her mouth opening to him in response he drew her closer and drowned in her warmth, her moistness and her flesh. As he always did.

"What are you going to do?" he asked her later. They were lying on the bed, holding each other loosely as if they wanted to hold on to the touch of each other a little longer.

Anna sighed. "I'm not sure. I am certain the two officers Karin eavesdropped on in the sauna are the same ones that have been sitting down here in the dining room these last few days."

"But they are only low ranking officers," af Klint said. "They can't be dangerous to the king."

"No. At least not as long as they don't just shoot him or something." Anna agreed. "But they might lead me to someone a little higher up."

Eric lifted an eyebrow, quite satisfied with his moderate reaction. "Are you going to seduce one of them?"

Anna giggled and started to stroke his back. "Actually I was thinking of just following them. Or have them followed. I think I am going to try and find one of my old contacts."

Eric liked that. "Good. I'd be a lot calmer if you weren't in this all on your own."

Anna smiled. It wasn't as easy as that, however.

She could not really be sure which of her old contacts were still loyal to the king, or if they'd started to side with the coup makers.

"It's not even sure they will be eating here tonight," she said after a while.

"So are you hungry? Because I am starved."

It was, however, Bosun Carl Tapper who eventually followed the two young officers while Anna and Eric ate their dinner without even getting a glimpse of the potential traitors. The bosun had stayed behind at the bathing house after Anna had left, stayed behind, as Karin lovingly had put it, to be thoroughly taken care of as well as to be rid of that monstrous beard of his.

"But it keeps me warm at sea, the beard does," Tapper tried, although he knew he did not stand a chance.

Karin only smiled at him while she rubbed the wet sponge softly over his chest. He was sitting in a tub of warm water, feeling positively blissful. The young woman leaned over him, her head only inches from his face. He could see her small firm breasts through the thin cloth of her wet dress.

"You smell very sweet," he said. Then he blushed.

She brushed his ear with her lips and whispered, "Just wait until you get to taste me." Watching him blush deeper yet, she moved back only to return with a shaving knife. "So let's see how you really look."

She had just finished shaving him and was admiring his clean face when Dillquist and Winther entered and sat down on the wooden bench nearest the stove.

"Look," Karin whispered, her face very close to Tapper's. "Here they are."

Tapper turned his head slowly as to kiss the side of her neck while he watched the two officers. They were too far away to be overheard, still Tapper spoke in a low voice as well. "We cannot send anyone to Anna, can we?"

Karin shook her head. "You could go, perhaps, but who knows how long they'll stay here? You might miss them."

"Do you think I should try to follow them when they leave?"

"I think that's what Anna would have done."

Tapper chuckled. "I think she'd rather tried to seduce them right here."

Karin's eyes widened. "She would?"

Tapper nodded. "She hasn't much shame she doesn't." He watched her expression change.

"What's the matter?" he asked.

Karin hesitated. "Carl, I shouldn't ask... But...,"

she blushed.

"You want to know if I..?" Tapper smiled at her. "I haven't. But I know others of my boat's crew who have..."

"Oh. But doesn't it bother the gunner? They are together now, aren't they?"

Tapper considered this. "I am not sure," he said ultimately. "I think it might bother him some. But I guess he just loves her..."

"Do you love me, Carl?"

"Aye," answered Tapper, realizing that he really did. "Aye, I do."

Two hours later Dillquist and Winther left, followed by Tapper, who felt all spongy after having been in the sauna for so long. He still wasn't sure if this spy business was a good idea, but neither he or Karin had been able to think up a better plan of action. So follow them he did, trying to keep as great a distance between them and himself as possible. It helped that it was dark outside, the street only being lit by the occasional lantern above a door or a glowing window.

Tapper felt sweaty, partly because his body was still hot from the sauna, partly because of the excitement. He only wished he had a real weapon. Being virtually decommissioned for the winter season, he only had his own sailor's knife which he of course carried at all times. But those traitors could very well have pistols or worse, perhaps a garrote? He shuddered. If they realized that he was following them, they might feel threatened and... Tapper pushed the thought away. They were, after all, in the middle of the city and there were other people around. Surely they would not want to attract any further attention by starting a fight.

When they reached the old town with its narrow streets and high buildings, Tapper had to keep closer to the two men in order not to lose them. There were fewer people here as well. He tried to keep track of where he was going, but soon he felt increasingly lost. He was a sailor, after all, and being on land was awkward enough without having to navigate this maze of narrow streets and alleys. He wished he had a compass. But he would not be able to see it in this poor light anyway. And a bosun was not supposed to navigate at all, that was what officers were for.

Tapper moved round the corner of a building just in time to see Dillquist and Winther disappear into a doorway. Carefully he followed, trying to make as little sound as possible. The door looked like it belonged to a shop, but there was nothing in the window next to it that would reveal what kind. Tapper peered though the window, but it was too dirty and it was dark inside. He hesitated. Going in after them was probably dangerous. At the very least it was stupid. Still, Tapper thought, he might just have a tiny look through the door? He could not just go home, could he? What would Anna think of him, surely she would have gone in without another thought?

Tapper eased the door open carefully and entered the building. Stopping directly inside the door, he listened. There was nothing. He took another step forward, then hesitated. He had a feeling that he wasn't alone. There was a movement in the air to his side. He turned towards it when something hard hit him over the side of his head and everything went black.

Chapter 11 – Inquiries

The next morning, Anna and Eric were having breakfast in the inn's dining room when an obviously disheveled Karin burst through the door. She looked searchingly around the room and seeing the couple at their table, her face lit up with relief.

"Karin," Anna cried. "Over here. Come and have a seat."

Eric rose from his seat and held out a chair for her. Seeing the girl's unhappy expression, Anna took her hand and asked: "What's wrong, Karin?"

Karin gulped and tears started to roll down her cheeks. "It's Carl... He..." she swallowed. "He did not come back yesterday," she said finally.

"He didn't come back?" Anna asked, patting her hand.

Karin wiped away her tears with the back of her hand, trying to pull herself together.

"Why don't you start from the beginning?" Eric said softly.

Karin nodded. "Well, after you had left the sauna yesterday," she looked at Anna who smiled encouragingly. "He stayed behind for a while... To take a bath." A sob escaped her throat. "Then those men came again."

"They did?" Anna's eyes widened.

"Yes. They stayed perhaps for an hour. We couldn't hear what they were saying, they sat on the opposite side of the room, and there was another girl there so I could not attend to them without it being... Suspicious?"

Anna nodded.

"We didn't really know what to do. Carl first wanted to send for you or go himself, but we were afraid they would leave before you came and then we would have lost them again, wouldn't we?"

"Yes. So Tapper followed them by himself?" Anna asked.

Karin blinked. "He said he would only find out where they went and then come back to the bathing house. But he never did." She looked at Anna. "He did not come here, did he?"

"No," Anna said. "He didn't. I'm sorry."

Karin covered her face with her hands and started to sob again.

"We'll take her up to our rooms," Anna said to Eric in a low voice. "You take care of her. Then I'll go and find Tapper."

Eric af Klint raised an eyebrow. "How are you going to do that?"

Anna smiled. "Clandestinely," she replied.

Captain Baker paced his quarterdeck, feeling utterly useless. It was a little warmer now and work aboard the frigate had been resumed as usual. There were men aloft, clearing the sails and rigging from ice and repairing damage to blocks and fastenings. Still the ice was thick and solid for several miles until more open water could be had. That fact was annoying enough – a sailor does not want to be stuck anywhere by any force other than his own doing. But the worst of it was that he had no communication at all with the capital. There had been no word from the embassy. He had no idea what was going on and he was getting tired of it.

Baker saw the first lieutenant ascending the ladder from the gun deck and called him over.

"A word, Mr. Reeman, if you please."

"Sir?"

"Ah, well. I am going into Stockholm again, Mr. Reeman. You will have the ship during my absence."

"Aye aye, sir."

The trip into the capital was much easier than the arduous ride the other way after his last visit. There was no blizzard this time, he could clearly see the tracks of sleighs, carriages and horses, and the white landscape was positively aglitter in the sunlight. There were even other travelers on the road. In fact there were so many that Baker had to slow down several times when met by big cargo sledges, drawn by six horses and loaded with huge amounts of wood, barrels or crates.

Baker passed the boatman's cottage where he had spent the night during the winter storm. He saw no-one and didn't want to be delayed by stopping by anyway. Perhaps on the way back, he thought.

Finally stopping at an inn close to the town port, he gulped down some light beer and ate a piece of bread with some suspicious glutinous substance smeared all over it. There was some commotion at the town port that made him curious. Several soldiers were standing together with two men in gray greatcoats, apparently having some agitated discussion. Not able to understand what was being said, Baker shrugged and mounted his horse in order to proceed through the port into the town. But he was stopped by one of the gray clad men.

"Who are you, sir?"

"I am a post captain of the British navy here to see my ambassador," Baker replied, trying to look commanding.

The gray clad man considered that, but didn't look like he was particularly impressed. Baker started to become impatient.

"Look, here, I don't know who you are and what

your business is, but the captain of an allied warship is essentially a diplomat. Are you aware of that at all?"

The gray man looked him right into the eyes and smiled wearily.

"That might be true. Still, we have to protect our king. A foreign military presence could, perhaps, complicate things..."

"I'm not a military presence. I am only one man!"

The gray man laughed unexpectedly.

"You may be one man, but you are also a symbol. Still, I will let you pass. Please be careful, though."

Baker raised his hand to his hat and urged his horse forward, wondering what all this was about.

"Those two?" Gray laughed. "They aren't a threat to anyone except themselves."

Anna raised an eyebrow. "But you know who they are then?"

"Yes, of course. Dillquist and Winther. They have been looking for someone to help them throw over the king for weeks. They even talked to me." He chuckled.

"Oh. What did you tell them then?"

"Well, I told them there wasn't going to be a revolution if there isn't anyone to take command afterward. It's not just about getting rid of the king.

There must be order."

Anna sat quietly for a while, thinking, while she looked at Gray. There was something wrong with him. She couldn't tell what it was, but her instinct told her Gray wasn't completely honest. And usually her instincts didn't betray her.

"Do you have any idea where to find them?" she asked eventually.

"Of course I do." Gray looked at her questioningly. "But why do you want to know?"

Anna hesitated too long for Gray not to notice. Raising an eyebrow he smiled. "Look, if you want me to give you information, you will have to play along. How do those men concern you? You aren't secret police, are you?"

Anna sighed. "Of course not. Alright, I will tell you."

Half an hour later Anna and Gray arrived at the shop in the old town. Gray produced a pair of pistols from under his greatcoat, checked their priming and handed one of them to Anna. Carefully, he pried the door open and they entered, pistols cocked and ready.

There wasn't much light inside the shop what with the window dirty and small, so they waited for their eyes to adjust to the twilight before they moved further. Perhaps they should have brought a lantern,

Anna thought. She shrugged and hurried after Gray who was about to disappear through another door in the back of the room.

"There is nobody here," Anna said, disappointed, after they had finished searching the shop.

"No," replied Gray. He had found a candle at last and was busy lighting it. Anna blinked when the flame came alive, then they started to look around more thoroughly.

"Is this blood?" she asked, having discovered several small stains on the wooden floor planks near the door.

Gray held the candle to the stains and put a finger into the sticky substance. "Yes, and it's not completely dry yet. Somebody was here until quite recently."

"Damn," Anna burst out.

Captain Baker was once again sitting opposite Ambassador Merry. Trying to calm down, he took a sip of his port.

"Ambassador Merry, sir," he started, then hesitated, coughing. "Do you have any idea as to what is going on in this country?"

The ambassador frowned. "Well, my dear captain, frankly, no." He rose from his chair and started to pace the room.

"There is some news about rebel troops on their way to Stockholm from Karlstad. There is also word of another conspiracy right here in the capital."

"Any names?" Baker inquired.

"No. Well, yes. The rebel troops are led by Adlersparre, a general, I think."

Captain Baker wished the ambassador would sit down, this pacing about made it difficult to think. But Merry went over to the drink cabinet and filled his glass, looking at Baker questioningly. Baker shook his head and raised his glass, showing it still being half full. Shrugging, the ambassador returned to his desk and, thank God, sat down.

"Anything I can do, sir?" Baker asked.

Merry considered that. "Well, your ship can't. But perhaps..."

"Yes?"

"You do have some Swedish acquaintances? From last summer, do you not?"

Baker nodded. "Yes, a gunboat squadron commander... But I can't see..."

"Meet him anyway. Just ask if he knows anything, will you?

"Of course, sir... But..."

"Yes?"

"Well, I think it would be easier if I had a reason to call on him."

Merry raised an eyebrow. "And do you have anything in particular in mind?"

"As a matter of fact I do. We... That is, the Royal Navy, owes him a share of prize money."

Chapter 12 – Before the Storm

"He is probably dead," Karin sobbed. She was sitting on Anna's bed at her room at Beckens inn, her head in her hands. Eric af Klind stood at the window, looking out, not really knowing what to do with the sobbing girl.

Anna, who had returned empty-handed from her rescue mission, sat next to Karin, one arm around the girl's slender body, comforting her. Of course, there was the probability of him indeed being dead. But she didn't really think so.

"Now, my dear, please don't fret so much. There wasn't nearly enough blood for him being seriously hurt, let alone dead."

Karin wasn't convinced. "They may have taken him away and killed him somewhere else..." she cried.

That was, of course, a possibility Anna had to admit. But she had a feeling that Dillquist and Winther wouldn't take the risk of attracting attention by killing someone. Also they had no idea why Tapper was following them in the first place, which would make them want to question him rather than kill him. At least question him first and perhaps kill him later.

Anna thought about Gray. Talking to him might have been a mistake. The man was definitely not completely honest. Christ, he even admitted having talked to the two revolutionaries.

And there was so little time. Gray had filled her in about the ongoing revolution – or coup d'état. In about a week Adlersparre's troops would arrive in Stockholm. The king was planning to make a stand in Norrköping – or try to move loyal troops to the capital from there – which alternative was the most probable, Gray did not know – or tell.

But there was something else. Something Gray had not told her. And unfortunately, there was no way for her to ever find out. She almost chuckled at the memory.

Anna had met Gray shortly before the war. He was a dark handsome man and he had this mysterious flair around him that attracted her immensely. And he had immediately sensed her talent for clandestine work. He taught her everything she needed to know, which wasn't much as most of it came to her by instinct.

And of course she had tried to seduce him. But failed. Failed most thoroughly and completely, standing naked in front of him, flushed with anger and desire, while he stood unimpressed, smiling at her. Then he had told her his secret. Gray wasn't attracted to women at all.

They had worked well together since, but Anna always felt unsure of him, because her most effective weapon she could not use against him.

She pushed away the thought, returning her focus to the problem at hand.

"Eric?" she said softly.

He turned towards her and looked into her eyes, seeing something there he hadn't seen before. Insecurity? Doubt? Then it passed and she looked as confident as ever.

"Yes, dear?"

"Eric, I think we must let the police look for Tapper."

Erik nodded. "Yes. Your contact, he can't help?"

"He did help a lot. We found the shop, the blood, but there are no clues as to where then bosun has been taken. And Gray... My contact... He has other things on his mind. The revolution is perhaps only a week away..."

Eric's eyes widened. "Are you sure?"

"He is. There are rebel troops on their way here as we speak. And there might be another conspiracy right here in the capital."

"Oh?"

"Well, Gray didn't say anything about that, but I

know he is hiding something and he keeps saying these two officers, Dillquist and Winther, aren't dangerous because there isn't anyone to lead the country after the king is overthrown. But I think he is hiding something from me."

Eric looked at her quietly.

"...and that might just be that there are people who are planning to take over. I can't even rule out that he is one of them himself... And..."

Eric moved towards the bed and sat down next to her, putting his hands to her face. Her eyes had that expression again and he suddenly knew that she was completely at a loss.

"Anna," he started.

"No, Eric. I must do something. I cannot just sit here. But I have no idea what I should do."

Eric held her face between his hands and kissed her softly. "You will, just rest a little and it will all become clear."

Anna nodded. Pulling herself together, she turned her face to Karin who still was sobbing quietly. "Listen, darling, why don't we all go down to the dining room and have something to eat. That might cheer us up."

Charlotte and Johan Kuhlin were having coffee when the maid announced a visitor.

"A foreign officer he is, can't understand a word of what he is saying, but he left this." She held out a small card to the commander. Kuhlin took it and read it carefully. Then he smiled.

"It's our Captain Baker of course. Please let him in." Looking at his wife he continued, "It says he wants to discuss a naval matter. Perhaps we'll get our prize money after all."

Baker, all glittering gold and lace, post captain style, was shown in by a deeply blushing maid, seated comfortably and offered coffee.

"Unfortunately, my dear captain, we do not have any wine," Charlotte explained, "but if you want a tot of vodka in your coffee, you are very welcome to it."

Baker accepted the offer gladly, thankful for anything that would warm his deep frozen body.

"I do not at all fathom," he said, "how you can cope with this awful weather weeks and months on end."

Charlotte smiled at him. "It's probably only a question of getting used to it, dear captain."

Baker grunted.

Kuhlin, never having been a man of great patience, cleared his throat and started. "May I enquire, captain Baker, sir..."

"Ah, yes... The naval matter." Baker smiled. "As a matter of fact it is about the prize money from the

Russian brig you took last summer."

"Yes?"

"Well, I have been assured by our ambassador, here, that the money indeed will be forthcoming."

Kuhlin smiled. "Very good, thank you, sir. But I assume there are... Conditions?"

Baker frowned. "Why should there be?"

Kuhlin laughed. "Come, captain, you know that the Royal Navy does not send out post captains to distribute prize money. You want something in return, don't you?"

Baker laughed as well. "Alright, commander, you have seen through the plot. Yes, the ambassador does ask a slight favor in return..."

Kuhlin raised an eyebrow.

"...He...Well, he feels a little... Well... Left behind as far as intelligence is concerned."

"He does?"

"Er... Yes. Your country being, well, in a state of... Um..." his voice trailed off.

"Uncertainty?" Kuhlin offered.

"Yes, perhaps?"

"My dear captain, I am afraid I cannot help you much at all. I am quite at a loss myself and I am not even trying to get involved... As an officer I guess I must be loyal to whomever is in charge... So to speak..."

"Oh." Baker considered this. "So you do not at all have any idea about how this... Situation might develop?"

"No, sir, afraid not." Kuhlin hesitated for a moment. "However, there might be someone else you could talk to..."

"Ah, and who might that be?" Baker asked, intrigued.

Kuhlin suddenly was unsure if this was a good idea. He liked Baker, in a way, and he appreciated the prize money – indeed needed it quite desperately to get through the rest of the winter without having to cut down on things, like the maid or the coffee. But he didn't want to put Anna at risk either. Then he made a decision.

"Alright, sir... This is how we must do this. I will have to ask this person first. You might want to stay in town for the night, perhaps?"

Baker nodded. "I was planning on doing this anyway."

"Well then, tell me where you will be staying and I... Or... Well... Someone will contact you."

Baker rose and offered his hand. "That would be perfect. Thank you kindly, sir."

Anna, Karin and Eric were sitting in the dining room at Beckens inn when Kuhlin arrived. Eric, who was sitting with his back to the wall saw him first and called him to their table. Kuhlin sat down heavily, still wearing his greatcoat.

"What brings you here?" Anna asked.

Kuhlin frowned. "Captain Baker, from the English frigate," he replied.

"Oh. What does he want?"

"To give me my prize money, for one," Kuhlin explained. "And bargain for information."

Anna raised an eyebrow. "Information? What kind of information?"

"Intelligence, I guess. About the political situation... Well... What is to happen with the king..."

"Nothing is going to happen to the king," Anna said quietly.

They all looked at her questioningly. Anna blushed. "He is the king after all. He must be protected."

Eric af Klint sighed. "Look, Anna..."

She put her hand on his and squeezed it lightly. "Don't, Eric," she said softly. "Let's hear what the commander has to say."

Kuhlin coughed. "Well, Baker asked me for... Well, my opinion on the situation. But I..."

"You don't have any opinion," Anna chuckled.

"Right. I don't think officers should be involved in

politics. I am a sailor, not... Well."

"And you told the captain that much?"

"Yes, but then I came to think of you."

"And thought I might be willing to help the captain out?" She shook her head. "Why on earth should I do that?"

Commander Kuhlin blushed.

Bosun Tapper woke to complete darkness. He put his hand to his aching head instinctively, feeling the dried blood in his hair. He swore silently. How stupid was this then, he thought. After decades of service in the navy he had let himself be drawn into some completely insane clandestine operation, something he had no expertise in whatsoever. And what had been the result? Misery. That's what it was.

He tried to move his legs, finding them restrained by some sort of rope. At least it was rope, he thought, rope he knew something about. But he still couldn't move his legs. His arms were free though, which was odd. Why would one only tie the legs of a man? Surely he must be able to free himself eventually? He felt the rope with his hands for the knot. Surely there must be a knot?

There wasn't. Instead there was a splice... Two splices... And a padlock. Tapper groaned. What a devious contraption. Sure, he might be able to work the splice free, if he had some sort of pointed tool, but not with his fingers alone. He felt for his knife, but of course it was gone. Sighing, he leaned back against the wall and tried to think.

And he thought of Karin. Her slender body, her delicious smell and the steamy heat of the sauna. Closing his eyes he tried to push away the thought. If he couldn't concentrate he might very well never get out of here alive and see her again. He would then never be able to touch her soft skin or kiss her moist lips and... Tapper groaned again. Pulling himself together he tried to move along the wall, feeling for anything that could be helpful, as a clue or as a device to escape.

It was tedious work. He could only move by dragging his body along the wall, using his tied legs and arms in some sort of crab-wise movement. He didn't dare move away from it as he didn't have any idea how big the room was or what was in it. Hugging the wall felt safest. The wall itself felt cold, almost moist. It also felt rugged, like raw stones or perhaps brick. An underground room then, some sort of cellar or basement, Tapper thought. He might still be in the same building, the shop, but of course he couldn't be sure. Having no idea how long he had been unconscious, he might have been moved elsewhere.

Tapper's hands started to get sore from the uneven surface of the wall. Cursing, he continued. At last he found something that felt different. Wood. A door frame? Tapper hauled himself up against the cold stones, moving his hands along the wood. Yes, there was a door. He put his back against it, pushing. The door creaked, but did not move. Groaning, he examined it further. The hinges were on the outside and there was no handle. Or was there? What was this? A cabin hook? Yes, indeed. Tapper felt a sudden sting of elation. If he could work free this thing he might use its point to work free that splice.

Chapter 13 – Preparations

Captain Baker was just about to go to bed when a messenger knocked at the door, informing him there was a lady visitor for him. Baker, intrigued, put his uniform coat back on and followed the messenger downstairs. The lady, having requested privacy, had been ushered into the drawing room.

Anna stood with her back towards the door when Baker entered. Turning around slowly she smiled and said: "Well, captain, do you remember me at all?"

Baker did of course remember her perfectly well. He almost blushed as he realized that she wore exactly the same dress as when he first had seen her at the theater. The cleavage was exactly as revealing, too. Baker forced his gaze to lift to her smiling eyes.

"Oh, I do indeed, miss..."

"Anna."

"Of course, yes... Um... I am delighted, naturally..." his voice trailed off.

Anna laughed. "You have no idea why I am here, do you?" She glided towards him and put one of her hands on his arm. "Will you perhaps order some tea for us? Then I will tell you."

Baker, feeling slightly dazed, cleared his throat

and walked towards the door. Anna, a cunning smirk on her face turned back to the sofa and sat down, dress rustling. She actually had missed this quite a lot. Being with Eric had pushed it away for a while, she even had thought she might be able to settle down with him on his estate. But these last days had stirred her up again and she now knew that she was too much an adventuress to ever be locked up in a cage by one single man – even if it was by her own choice and even if she loved that man.

She looked at the British captain coming back through the door, feeling the air of confidence around him, the power of command, the sheer masculinity. But also the insecurity of being alone with her in that room and the fact that he so clearly was attracted to her – all that made her body tingle with excitement.

"Please sit down with me, captain," she said, patting the spot next to her on the sofa.

Baker hesitated only for a second, then sat down stiffly, turning his upper body towards her. He coughed. "Um... I think the tea will be here in a minute, miss Anna..."

"I'm in no hurry, dear captain," Anna replied calmly, looking straight into his eyes.

"Right. Well, do you care to tell me then, why you are here?"

Anna smiled at him. "I think we will wait for the tea first. We would not want to be disturbed, I think."

"Oh?" Baker's eyes went wide.

Anna chuckled, opening her mouth to say something when the door opened and a maid appeared.

The tea served at last, cups in their hands and having taken their first sips, Anna spoke again.

"So, my dear captain, you have been visiting an old friend of mine this afternoon..."

"Oh. Yes, Commander Kuhlin..." Baker hesitated.

"And you were told he needed to talk to someone who might be able to help you?"

Baker's face flushed red. "Um... Miss I am sorry, but this business..."

Anna put her hand softly on his arm. "That someone is me, captain."

Baker almost dropped his teacup. His mouth fell open and he gaped at her for a while. Finally pulling himself together he coughed.

"You are the one who...?"

"I have certain dealings with people who work in intelligence, captain."

Baker considered this. "Well, I am sorry, miss. I had no idea."

Anna looked into his eyes and smiled, seeing the

change. There was still desire in those eyes and admiration, but now there was more. Perhaps respect. Or amazement.

"Captain, pray tell me what you want to know."

"Well, it's really the ambassador who wants to know, miss. But of course I want to too, you see I have this ship at Dalarö, frozen in the ice and more or less unable to leave."

Anna nodded patiently.

"Yes, and we, that is the ambassador of course, and I, we don't know a thing about what is going on in this country and who will be in charge in a few weeks."

Anna sighed. "My dear captain... I fully understand your situation. However, the problem is, nobody knows very much right now. There are lots of rumors. There are people who talk about revolution. And there are, apparently, rebel troops on their way to Stockholm."

Baker stiffened. "That rumor is true then?"

"It is definitely true," Anna confirmed.

"So there will be a civil war?"

"Perhaps. It all depends on the king."

Baker looked at her questioningly. "And what is the king going to do?"

Anna chuckled. "No-one really knows."

"He doesn't tell?"

"Oh he does. But he tells different things to different people. And the people who tell these things to other people, like me or you, do not necessarily tell us the same thing the king told them."

Baker raised an eyebrow. "I am not entirely sure if I follow you…"

Anna laughed. "I'm sorry, captain. The clandestine world is not always easy to understand. Subterfuge and deception are a natural part of it. Many people in this line of work do not tell the truth habitually or only parts of it."

"I see. So you claim there are no sources entirely to be trusted?"

Anna smiled. "Exactly. One of my closest contacts, for example, he might as well be loyal to the king or a rebel. You won't be able to tell until the last minute."

Baker looked increasingly puzzled. Anna, seeing that, squeezed his arm lightly. "Do you not find me helpful, dear captain?"

Baker wondered if her hand had been on his arm during the whole conversation. It probably had. Suddenly it felt hot on his sleeve.

"Captain?"

Baker pulled himself together. "Sorry, miss."

"Can I ask you a favor?"

"Of course," Baker replied instinctively.

"Will you take me to Dalarö and show me your ship?"

Baker blushed deeply, his mouth agape in astonishment.

Bosun Tapper swore. This hook wasn't nearly as pointed as he had wished. In fact it almost wasn't any help at all. He had worked hard for at least half an hour but only managed to free a few strands of the splice. This would take all day – or night for that matter, and his fingers were already sore and tired. He sighed and stopped working for a while. Surely they would not just leave him down here to rot? Perhaps it would be better to rest and save his strength until they came back for him.

Tapper thought about Karin again. She must be terribly worried by now. Hopefully, she would have gone for help. Perhaps talked to Anna or Kuhlin. They might already be out looking for him. But of course, how were they supposed to find him here? As far as they were concerned he could be absolutely anywhere.

Then his body tensed. There was a noise. Could it be a rat? Something was shuffling outside the door. Tapper pressed himself against the wall close to the door. It was a pity it opened outwards, he thought.

Clasping the hook in his hand he waited. There was a rustle as someone moved the bolt on the outside of the door. Creaking as the heavy door swung outwards. Tapper closed his eyes in order not to be blinded by the light from the lantern he expected his visitor to carry, then opened them slowly again.

He saw the back of a man in a gray greatcoat, holding a lit lantern in his left hand and a pistol in his right. The man was peering into the room, looking for him against the far wall. The man grunted, then said: "I know you are here, bosun, don't play games."

Tapper had been prepared to haul himself up and throw his body against the man, hoping to bring down the lantern in the process. In darkness, he thought he might have had a chance. But something made him change his mind. What had the man just said?

"Why did you call me bosun?" he said softly.

The man startled and turned around, pistol at the ready. When he saw Tapper still on the floor he relaxed.

"Because that's what you are, Mr. Tapper, are you not?"

"Who are you?" Tapper asked. "You are not one of the men who put me in here."

The man laughed. "No, I'm not. I am the man who

might get you out of here, if you will be so kind as to co-operate."

"Co-operate about what?" Tapper asked carefully.

"Let's get you out of here and I'll tell you."

The man put his pistol into the pocket of his coat and produced a knife, cut the rope around Tapper's legs, then offered the bosun his hand. Tapper took it and rose carefully. He groaned. "I do feel a bit stiff," he said.

Captain Baker hadn't been this nervous for a long time. He was riding his horse slowly through the glittering winter landscape, ever so often casting a glance at the woman on the horse alongside. Anna wore a hooded fur cape that covered her completely as well as half of the tiny Nordic horse. Only her face was visible, deliciously flushed with red from the cold air stinging her skin. A slight smile played around her mouth as she was well aware of the captain's glances.

Baker wondered why he had agreed to her request to visit his ship. It probably wasn't a good idea at all. A warship, frozen in the ice, with no proper heating definitely wasn't the right place for a woman to be. And Dalarö was far enough from Stockholm to render it impossible to return home the same day. But of course, that was probably why he had agreed to this in the first place. He would have to let her stay on the ship over night, and that thought intrigued him. It held possibilities indeed.

Anna, on the other hand, or horse, was having almost the same thought. For her, the British captain held possibilities in several ways. He was a handsome, dashing man for one, but most of all he had a powerful warship under his command. A warship, furthermore, belonging to a powerful country, a country which not only ruled the oceans of the world, but also was a bitter enemy of France. As was the king of Sweden. Seeing the captain glance at her again, she smiled.

They arrived at Dalarö shortly after sunset, riding their horses all the way onto the ice to the frigate. Lieutenant Reeman, who was officer of the deck, greeted them with a puzzled expression on his face.

"Welcome back, sir. Um... And..."

"Thank you, Mr. Reeman. Now, as you can see we have a visitor tonight, Miss Anna Wetterstrand. Pray send word to the galley to prepare a suitable supper in, say, one hour?"

"Aye aye, sir." Reeman disappeared. Baker offered Anna his arm. "I think, it being all dark, we will make the tour of the ship tomorrow morning? And now proceed directly into the great cabin?"

"Of course, you are the captain," Anna smiled.

It wasn't exactly warm in the great cabin. Extending over the complete width of the ship it was by far the biggest room aboard. Its backside was covered by big windows which, had it not been dark, would have presented a spectacular view over the snowy islands surrounding the anchorage. Along the windows stretched a cushioned bench which after the long ride on horseback seemed utterly inviting.

There was even a table and a couple of chairs as well as a desk. Against the forward bulkhead, on either side, were two small cabins, separated by walls of canvas covered wooden frames.

"The one on the port side is my sleeping cabin," Baker explained. "Which I, of course, will vacate for you to use."

Anna smiled at him, her hand squeezing his arm slightly. "Thank you, captain."

"Um, yes, on the other side is the chart room, where, well, the nautical charts are kept."

Anna nodded.

"Well now, miss, would you like to sit with me on the bench there and we will have some wine?"

"Oh, yes please." Anna beamed. She took off her cape, putting it on the bench and sat down next to it. Immediately she felt chilly.

"It's quite cold in here, don't you think?" she

asked.

Captain Baker nodded. "Yes, I am sorry about that. But it is not easy to warm up a wooden ship. We have the braziers of course, but the cabin is big and the hull... Well the walls are not very thick." He hesitated. "Perhaps I should not have brought you here. It is really not a place for a woman."

Anna sighed. "Dear captain. It was me who wanted to come here. So don't worry. Just get us the wine you promised and then we will sit here and pull this cape around us for warmth."

Baker swallowed. "Very well, I will get the wine."

"I really was starving," Tapper said to the man on the opposite side of the table as he dug into his stew. They sat in one of the numerous small taverns of the old town and the man who had brought Tapper here was, of course, Gray.

Tapper gulped down the rest of his beer and wiped his mouth with his sleeve. "Now, mister, what do you want me to help you with?" he asked.

Gray smiled at him. "Are you not at all curious about how I found you down there?"

Tapper frowned. "Yes, perhaps I am. But I'm yet more interested to know what you want from me. I'm a sailor, mister, not a spy."

"I know that, bosun. Yet you were definitely

spying recently or you wouldn't have been down there..."

Tapper blushed. "Alright, but it wasn't really for my own sake. I was..." he stopped himself.

"You were trying to help Miss Anna, were you not?"

Tapper's mouth fell open. "What do you know about her?"

Gray took a sip of his beer. Indicating Tapper's empty mug he said: "You want another one, bosun?"

"I'd rather have you answer my question."

Gray laughed. "All right, bosun. Let me just make this clear: in this line of work, we do not tell people too much. It isn't good for us and it isn't good for them, either. So just be assured that I know Miss Anna very well. Actually she came to me asking for help finding you."

Tapper's eyes widened. "She did? Why isn't she with you then?"

Gray shrugged. "We didn't find you so she went to turn the case over to the police."

"But then you found me..."

"Not really. I knew where you were all along."

Tapper took a deep breath. He was beginning to get angry with this man. "Listen, mister, if you did know it all the time, why did you let me rot down there for so long? Why didn't you get me out right away?"

Gray looked at him calmly. "Two reasons: first I needed to make sure your two rebels weren't around. Second: I couldn't have Anna around either."

"Why the hell not." Tapper almost shouted.

"Because I need her to think you are not a free man."

Tapper sat speechless.

"Look, bosun, are you sure you don't want another beer?"

Chapter 14 – Allies

Captain Baker felt hot, despite the chilly air in the great cabin of HMS Tartar. He felt hot, partly because he was completely at a loss with himself and this situation, partly because he was sitting close to a lovely woman under a great furry cape, only heads and arms sticking out, sipping claret. He felt the closeness of Anna's body, her warmth, her scent and every time he glanced at her he saw her white throat, and he wanted to trace the line of it down under the edge of the cape towards what he knew was there.

He took another sip of wine, trying to calm down. When he looked up again he saw her smiling at him. "Tell me, captain, what are you thinking? You have suddenly become so quiet."

Baker blushed. "Oh... I... Um. I was just enjoying the wine and the... Um... Company."

Anna looked at him, her eyes wide. And so deep, Baker thought, so deep he wanted to find out if there ever was a bottom. He moved his face closer to hers.

"Do you enjoy my company, then?" Anna said in a low voice, her eyes still on his.

Baker put his glass down on the bench next to him and lifted both his hands towards her face. Softly he put them against her cheeks, fingertips just brushing her ears. "You have the most intriguing eyes I've ever seen," he said. "They are bottomless, they make me want to drown in them."

Anna opened her mouth slightly, moistening her lips with the tip of her tongue.

"Please do drown, captain," she whispered.

Baker put his lips against hers, still looking into her eyes. Then he closed his own as their mouths melted together in a deep kiss. He let his hands slide down the sides of her neck until he was under the cape, feeling her collarbones, the soft skin above her breasts, then the round flesh itself, until stopped by the fabric of her dress.

He gasped into her mouth as he felt her hands on him, feeling their way over his uniform, finding him ready and caressing him through the fabric of his breeches. Pulling her towards him, he lowered his face into her throat, working at the complicated lacing on the back of her dress.

Moaning softly, Anna pushed him backwards until he ended up on the bench with her on top of him. Her hands were still working on his breeches, finally releasing him. She held him, squeezing him softly as he freed her upper curves and buried himself into her soft white flesh.

Later, they lay exhausted under the cape, breathing the sweet smell of their lovemaking, still touching each other as to not let the magic of the moment disappear.

Baker started to speak first. "Miss Anna... I... You are amazing..."

He felt Anna's hand touch his face. "I know."

He almost heard her smile. Baker continued. "Ever since I saw you at the theater I haven't been able to stop thinking of you."

"I know," Anna said again.

Baker hesitated. He really had no idea what to do with this woman. She was so utterly sweet and delicious and passionate, he had never met the like before. Not in the upper circles of British society. Well, that perhaps was to be expected, but not in the taverns of the seaside towns of the world either. Well, yes, there were passionate women in those taverns, but none had ever captured him with their eyes like this. At the same time, however, he realized that there was no future in this at all. He was a post captain in the Royal Navy, what was he supposed to do?

Anna's hand was still touching his face. Softly, deliciously. Baker sighed. "Miss..."

"Will you not call me Anna?" she whispered into his ear.

"Of course... Anna. Um, I wonder... how long... Um."

"How long until dinner?" Anna moved her face towards his until Baker could feel her breath against his lips.

"No." Baker sighed. "That dinner is probably cold long since... Didn't you hear the knock on the door?"

"Oh," Anna stuck out her tongue and touched his upper lip with the tip of her tongue.

Baker shivered. "Fortunately they'd never dare come in without permission. What I meant was; how long will I have the pleasure of your company?"

"Quite a while my dear," she said, tongue playing over his lower lip.

"You see, I'd very much like you to sail me to Norrköping."

Baker gasped in astonishment, then in delight as he felt her mount him again.

Eric af Klint sat alone in the dining room at Beckens inn, staring forlornly into a mug of ale when bosun Tapper entered. Eric, seeing him, almost jumped out of his chair. "Bosun Tapper! Christ, where have you been?!"

Tapper hastened to Eric's table and sat down heavily opposite of the gunner. "It's a long story," he sighed.

"I'm in no hurry, bosun," Eric replied, waving to the waiter for another beer. Tapper, however frowned. "Sorry, but I don't have time. Is Anna here?"

Erik shook his head.

"Where is she then?"

"I don't know." Eric took another sip at his beer. " She went off on some cloak-and-dagger-business and I did not ask her where to."

Tapper considered that. This was not going as it was supposed to and he didn't like it. For a moment he thought about confiding in the gunner, but Gray's voice was still in his head. It was too dangerous to tell people things these times. Especially officers. Not that he didn't trust Eric, after all they had sailed together and fought together for a season. Still, there were other things to consider. Karin for example. He sighed and gulped down a considerable part of his beer. Wiping his mouth with the back of his sleeve he made his decision.

"Well, sir, I have to run. Must at least see Karin and tell her I am fine."

"Of course," Eric agreed. "She's supposed to be at work?"

"Aye," Tapper said, already on his way out.

He arrived at the bathing house half an hour later. Not bothering to take off his clothes he stormed right into the hot steamy sauna. Karin was just about to throw a bucket of water onto the hot stones above the stove in order to create steam that would make the air more moist and thus feel hotter than it really was. Turning as she heard him enter, she dropped the bucket and gasped in relief. "Carl," she cried and ran towards him, throwing her arms around him.

Tapper held her tight, his hands feeling her soft curves through the thin fabric of her linen gown.

"Karin," he whispered into her hair, feeling the moistness of her tears against his neck.

The heat of the sauna felt intense, but he didn't care. He could have stood like this and held her for the rest of his life. But then he heard Gray's voice in his head again. Softly, he pushed the girl back at arm's length and looked her in the eyes. "Karin," he said softly. "I must go away for a while."

"What?" her eyes widened. "But you just came back." Her voice faltered. "Where have you been, what happened?"

"Please, darling. I can't tell you. It's for your own good."

"But..."

"Please. Trust me. I must go and help Anna."

"Oh." Karin blushed.

"No, Karin, please..." Tapper felt at a loss. "Listen, I..." He saw her eyes moisten. Softly he took her face between his hands and kissed her.

"I love you, Karin. Please trust me."

She nodded, her eyes closed.

General Döbeln sat in a poorly heated fisherman's hut on one of the many islands overlooking the sea between Åland and the Finnish mainland. However, it was not the sea he was staring at now, but a foggy stretch of whiteness, ice and sky blurred together. He blinked, trying to make out some different shape or colour in all this whiteness, something that could indicate that the Russians were finally coming.

There had been reports of some scouting parties visible far out, but no sign of the main army. And it was getting late, the weather becoming warmer all the time. If they were to come at all, they must come any day now, Döbeln thought.

He was interrupted by a knock on the door and the entry of a young officer, carrying a dispatch bag.

"Ah, ensign Dillquist, you are back at last," Döbeln said.

"Yes, sir, sorry about the delay, but the situation in Stockholm..." his voice trailed off.

"Tell me about it."

"Well, the dispatches..."

"I'll read those later. Tell me in your own words," Döbeln demanded.

Dillquist cleared his throat. "Well, first there is

the revolution..."

"What revolution? The King is still the king, is he not?"

"Yes, sir. But there are rebel troops on their way from Karlstad and..."

Döbeln rose out of his chair. "Karlstad?" he cried. "That Adlersparre became a traitor at last!"

Dillquist said nothing to that.

"Well, continue!"

"Eh, yes and the king is said to be looking to Norrköping for help."

"Norrköping? But my army is much closer!" Döbeln frowned.

"Yes, sir, but there are the Russians to consider. It's all in the dispatches. Your orders, sir..."

"I know my orders. I am to defend Åland or die trying. Which I am going to do... The latter that is."

Bosun Tapper arrived at the Kuhlin's house half an hour after he left Karin. He wasn't really sure if Kuhlin was the right person to talk to, but frankly, there was no-one else. The gunner would help, of course, but he was just a gunner and Tapper instinctively looked for a person who could command a ship, if that was what was needed now.

He was served the usual coffee and vodka, before he even had a chance to talk. Then, sitting in front of the fireplace he put his request to the commander.

"Well, sir, I am sorry to bother you with this..." he blushed.

"Come on, bosun, out with it," Kuhlin smiled encouragingly

Tapper coughed. "You see, I know you don't want to become involved in this revolution business..."

"Indeed I won't." Kuhlin narrowed his eyes.

"...but, it's about Anna now."

"What about her? Surely she can fend for herself. Always has."

"Well, not in Turku last summer, sir..."

Kuhlin nodded. He and af Klint had saved her then. But that had been mostly a military operation, where the enemy was clearly defined.

"Go on," he said.

"Now, you see, I tried to help her a little during those last few days and got myself into a bit of trouble..." Tapper then told Kuhlin about his adventure.

"Oh." Kuhlin said. "And this Gray person, he thinks Anna is off getting herself into serious trouble?"

"Yes, sir."

"But can you trust him?"

"I don't know, sir. But if he is right, then Anna is in danger. If he is trying to trick me, well, I can't see what he would gain from that."

Kuhlin thought about that. Tapper was of course right. Anna was apparently siding with the wrong people in this mess and Gray didn't think he could convince her otherwise, or protect her himself, because he knew she would never trust him. Not on this. Kuhlin sighed deeply.

"Bosun, I really hate this. I really hate politics. But I agree that we should try to help her."

"Thank you, sir". Tapper looked relieved.

"Still, bosun, how on earth are we to do that?"

"We need a boat I think," Tapper said.

"But the ice is still thick in the archipelago. We won't get out to sea."

"Then we must find a boat further south, sir."

Kuhlin nodded. "Or go the whole way by land. We need to talk to af Klint, I am sure he would want to come with us. And he has a sleigh."

Chapter 15 – Breaking Out

They began working at dawn the next morning. Baker had assembled his officers in the great cabin in order to discuss the operation. They were standing around the table on which lay a chart of the southern archipelago. Anna was sitting on the aft bench, listening to the discussion, a faint smile on her mouth.

"Any questions, gentlemen?" Baker asked after having explained his plan.

"Um, yes, sir, if you don't mind me…" the first lieutenant said.

"Pray go ahead, Mr. Reeman."

"Well, sir, this whole operation… Um… Is the ambassador involved at all. I mean, is it official?"

Baker's eyes narrowed. "I am the captain of a frigate, Mr. Reeman. When I have business it is always official."

"Of course, sir. No offense, sir." Reeman blushed.

"None taken. Still, I'd rather hear your questions about the specific operation at hand. That is, if there are any?"

There were none. Thus dismissed, the officers left the great cabin and went to instruct the crew. Captain Baker sat down besides Anna and took her hand in his.

"You are very attractive, when you are in command," she said softly, smiling at him.

"Do you think so?" Baker lowered his face towards her and kissed her, softly first, but then deeper, his arms now around her waist.

"Oh yes," she moaned.

Four hours later, they walked down onto the ice in order to inspect the progress of the operation. The ship's hands had drilled holes into the ice, ten yards apart and in two straight lines about one cable length from the ship's bows towards the open water which barely could be seen two nautical miles further to the southeast. The holes were big enough to take three charges of gunpowder each, sausages of canvas, filled with the explosive and equipped with slow-burning fuses.

Anna, her arm on the captain's looked up into his face, eyebrows raised. "Will this really work, my dear captain?"

Baker shrugged. "It better do or I will face serious depreciation of my authority." He smiled. "But let me explain how it is supposed to work. See, what we are trying to achieve is to break up the ice into floes a few yards across, and then push those floes under the ice to the sides in order to create a canal through which to tow the Tartar out to sea."

Anna nodded. "Have you done this before?"

"Never." Baker smiled. "But there is a first time for everything, is there not?"

Anna returned his smile. "Indeed, my dear captain, it is."

The first lieutenant appeared and lifted his hand to his hat. "We are ready to light the first charges, sir."

"Very good, Mr. Reeman. Get the people off the ice and then light the charges." He turned to Anna. "Come on, my dear, we need to go back to the ship."

Eric af Klint didn't like it. In fact, he was starting to despair. Sure, he had known it all along when he had given in and accepted his feelings for Anna. He had been sure that he would never be able to keep her for himself for any longer period of time. And so he had not tried to, either. But being in love does things to a man and it's not always easy to restrain oneself. Although he knew he must.

But now this. Not only did she take up her clandestine career again – that was only to be expected after all - but she did it out of vain loyalty to an idea that hadn't been real for years. Everybody knew that the king could not last if Sweden was to be saved as a nation. Still he had not said anything to her, being afraid he would push her away. He had decided to let her fly, hoping she would do the right thing and come back to him in the end. And she still might. If she survived this revolution, or coup d'état or whatever it was supposed to be called.

He sighed and looked at Kuhlin and Tapper. "Alright, of course we will go after her. There's no other way, is there?"

"No," Kuhlin replied. "Not if we want to keep our consciences clear."

"So where do we start?" Eric asked.

"Gray says she is going to Norrköping in order to save the king," Tapper said.

Eric af Klint groaned. "How is a single woman supposed to do that? Seduce every single rebel officer?"

"Not even Anna could do that," Kuhlin replied dryly.

"So how is she to save the king then? She isn't stupid, I am sure she has some sort of plan."

Kuhlin sat quietly for a while. Then his eyes brightened.

"Eric," he said. "Do you remember when we were at the theater?"

Eric nodded.

"And do you recall this British captain?"

"Yes..."

"He called on me, do you see? Wanted me to help

him with information. Of course I couldn't give him any, but I talked to Anna about it."

"Yes, I remember," Eric straightened up. "Do you mean she went to him anyway? Even though she told us she wouldn't?"

"I wonder." Kuhlin replied. "You did of course note the captain's reaction to her?"

"Of course, his eyes were all in her cleavage."

"So..."

Eric af Klint groaned again. "She would have him under her spell in no time at all."

Kuhlin nodded. "I think Anna literally commands a powerful frigate by now."

"And will use it to bring the king out of the country."

"So how do we stop her?" Tapper asked.

The explosions sounded amazingly dull, the sound muffled by the ice. Anna and Captain Baker stood in the bows of the frigate and watched the detonations throw up grayish white geysers of ice, snow and gunpowder. Then hands were scurrying down the gangplank, boat hooks and boarding pikes in their hands. With those they started to push broken floes under the edges of the surrounding ice. It was dangerous work, the floes being of different size, some of them big enough to require one or several men to step onto them in order to push them low and under the edge. Other floes were small enough to be easily pushed under by boat hooks. And then there were the medium sized ones, the most dangerous. Several times, men who stepped onto them made them capsize, ended up in the water and had to be pulled back by their shipmates, drenched and shivering of cold.

Still, after several hours of work, a canal appeared in the ice and the men were ordered to tow the frigate through it, all hands pulling the lines, including the officers and an insistent Miss Anna. The task completed, the ship was one cable length closer to the open water and the sun was setting.

"This is going to take a week," Captain Baker told Anna when they had supper in the great cabin.

"We don't have a week, my dear captain," Anna replied. "Not that I would mind being here a week," she added in a lower voice, her eyes on the captain's.

Baker swallowed. "There must be a faster method," he said.

Anna nodded. Putting her hand on his, she softly stroked his fingertips. "You will find it I am certain."

Baker smiled. "We could always use more gunpowder."

The next day they doubled the charges. Baker also ordered several lighter charges to be placed in random order between the straight lines marking the edge of the canal to be.

"Now, Mr. Reeman," Baker explained. "The general idea is that we might be able to confuse the ice enough – that is create small enough floes - not to be needing to push them under the edge at all."

"You mean tow Tartar right through the ice, sir?"

"Exactly. Now, Mr. Reeman see to the charges being set if you please."

The charges were set and detonated and there were yet higher geysers of white and gray, and as though by magic the ice in the canal was reduced to a grayish mush. That day, Tartar was towed one and a third nautical miles towards the open sea.

"We will be sailing tomorrow," Baker said, softly stroking Anna's naked back. They were lying in his swinging cot, a wooden box suspended on ropes from the ship's deck beams enabling him to sleep level even when the ship was heeling. The cot was quite small, but neither of them cared, their bodies pressed together tightly, both for warmth and from passion.

"Yes, that will be lovely," Anna whispered. "I haven't felt the motions of a ship for months."

"Do you like to sail?" he asked, his hand now in the small of her back, stroking the soft skin, occasionally moving up on the intriguing hills of her buttocks.

"I do like it very much. It gives me a great feeling of freedom. Like if I could go anywhere..." She sighed.

"You can go anywhere..." Baker replied. "Anywhere in the world." Then he put his other arm under her waist and slid her atop of him while his mouth tasted the sweet scent of her neck. Anna, moaning, parted her legs and let him enter her, softly biting into his earlobe.

Chapter 16 – Chase

The sleigh raced towards Dalarö as fast as the horses could run. All three men were wearing their uniforms, trying to give their endeavor an official look. They also carried weapons. Kuhlin and af Klint wore their swords, while Tapper had organized three pistols. Kuhlin had tried to pry out of him where from, but the bosun had only smiled at him. And frankly, Kuhlin didn't care. Organizing things was what petty officers were for in the navy, after all.

Traffic was light this day, thank God, but they still had to dodge the occasional cargo sled. Sometimes they had to slow down behind one of them until the road widened enough to enable them to pass.

When they neared the fort at Dalarö, Kuhlin pondered their options. He might just ask the commanding officer to lend him a few men, giving his mission a yet more official character. Or he could just pull up right to the frigate and ask for Anna. In any case, she would not like it.

He could see the fort now, with its flagpole. A perfect sailing wind, he thought, right from the northwest. Unusual, too.

Then the sleigh passed the highest point of the road and they started to descend to the seafront.

"Hey, where is the frigate?" Bosun Tapper burst out.

"It should be there with the other…" Kuhlin's mouth fell open. "What the hell is that?" He reined in the horses and looked sharply at the anchorage. There was a straight canal of mushy water right from it to the sea. And no frigate.

"Damnation!" swore Kuhlin.

"They've sailed right out of the ice," Tapper cried.

Eric af Klint just shook his head.

"Oh, this is so lovely!" Anna gasped. She stood on the quarterdeck of HMS Tartar, her furry cape tight around her, as well as one of Captain Baker's arms.

"Yes, indeed. There is nothing worse than a ship that cannot sail. I am so pleased to be in open water again," he agreed.

The frigate was sailing under full plain sail on a southwesterly course, out to sea, away from the ice and the dangers of submerged rocks and barely visible skerries.

Hands were tending the rigging, repairing some minor damages that had not been noticed with the sails furled and the rigging unused during the stay in the ice. In the waist of the ship others were tending to the ship's boats or just huddling away from the wind. For even though it wasn't nearly as freezing as when they came here, it was still winter and the northerly wind was bitterly cold.

"How long do you think it will take?" Anna asked.

Baker looked up at the full sails of his ship for a moment, then turned his gaze back onto her face.

"How long do you want it to take?" he asked softly.

Anna actually blushed. Then she tightened her grip around his arm. "You shouldn't really ask me questions like that…"

Baker laughed. "Don't worry, my dear, we will get your king out. This is the Royal Navy, we can do anything."

Anna smiled at him.

"So what are we going to do now?" Tapper asked.

Commander Kuhlin looked at the anchorage in despair. This was simply incredible.

"I still can't believe it. It's more than two miles. It must have taken tons of gunpowder."

In fact, he was positively awed. Not so much at the fact that it had been done, as a seaman he acknowledged the scientific fact that it was possible. He had even heard about similar things having been done in the Arctic. But that had been in order to survive, in order to not have one's vessel crushed by the ice and sunk with all hands lost. A last desperate effort for survival. But this was something different. No Swedish captain would even have thought about it. There was definitely something admirable about the British. At least their sailors. They did not find anything impossible, and with that state of mind probably nothing was. Kuhlin pulled himself together.

"Well, we need to continue south along the coast and find a place that is ice-free and where we can get ourselves a boat."

"A boat that is faster than a frigate?" Tapper asked.

Kuhlin shrugged. "Any boat. Even if it's not faster, we might be able to cut her off by sailing inshore, closer to the rocks. I am sure, captain Baker will take his ship far out to sea in order to keep her out of danger."

The three men climbed back on the sleigh and urged the horses forward, following the coastal road south.

On another road, another man made his way south on horseback. Carrying only a bag of dispatches, like the one Dillquist brought to Åland, sub-lieutenant Winther was on his third horse since he left the capital, only having stopped to eat and sleep for four hours. Despite being dead tired, he was committed to continue to his destination without further delay.

Or the first of his possible destinations in any case. Because there were three of them - three places along the coast that might or might not be ice-free. Winther desperately hoped the first one would be. Then he could get himself a room in a boarding house at the harbour, have a good meal, some ale and perhaps even a girl. And just wait.

Let there not be ice, he thought. Please let there not be ice.

But there was ice, and lots of it too. Groaning, Winther allowed himself two hours of rest until he continued south, on yet another new horse.

Kuhlin, af Klint and Tapper reached the small fishing village of Nynäs shortly after dusk. There was still enough light, what with the snow reflecting what the full moon threw at it, to see that there was some ice, but not too far out. Half a mile off the tiny harbour there was dark water, definitely open water.

"Let's find some place to spend the night," Kuhlin said. "Tomorrow we will get a boat that is small enough to be dragged over that ice until it can be sailed – and big enough to carry us where we want to go."

Tapper smiled. "That's the navy way."

Eric af Klint frowned. "Does the navy ever eat?"

The next morning they explored the harbour. There were actually a few fishing boats already dragged out over the ice and moored against the edge of it. After all, fishermen needed to fish to make a living, and when there was open water, they would try to get to it.

"So are we just going to steal one of those boats?" af Klint asked.

Kuhlin shook his head. "You mean borrow, like we did in Finland last summer when we rescued Anna in Turku?"

Eric af Klint smiled at the memory. That had been an exciting adventure. And a successful one as well. They had saved Anna right in the middle of Russian occupied territory and killed a Swedish traitor in the process.

"Well, there wasn't anyone around then," he said. "I don't think we can get our hands on a boat this easily here."

"Watch me," Kuhlin said, then turned to Tapper. "Bosun, get that pistol of yours primed and follow me.

"Aye aye, sir."

The three men closed on the biggest of the fishing boats. Two men were aboard her, mending nets. When the officers stopped next to their boat, the men looked up, a wary expression on their faces.

"Good day to you," Kuhlin said cheerfully.

The fishermen only nodded at him.

"Nice boat you have here," Kuhlin continued. "Looks quite seaworthy indeed."

"Aye, she is," the older of the fisherman replied, apparently being too proud of his vessel not to admit the fact.

"Now look, I am sorry, men, but I need to commandeer your fine vessel for a few days."

The older man rose to his feet. "You can't do that! It's my only way to make a living."

Kuhlin smiled at him, trying to calm him down. "I will do my very best to have the inshore fleet pay you. I'm not trying to take your boat away from you. But I really need it and I have the right to take it. So I will give you the choice. You can charter it to me, go with us yourselves and, hopefully be paid. Or we will take it by force."

The man stood silent for a while. "Consider it chartered, then," he said and shrugged.

"Very good. Eric, get aboard. Bosun, undo those mooring lines. You men, get the sails ready. There is not a minute to be lost."

Kuhlin stepped aboard the vessel and positioned himself at the tiller. He had to try very hard to suppress a grin. It felt so good to be in command of a vessel again, even if it only was a 25 foot fishing smack.

And it wasn't a bad boat either. Despite its size the small lug rigged vessel cleaved the choppy gray water of the Baltic nicely enough, its shallow draft enabling them to short-cut through inside passages and round rocks and headlands at biscuit-toss distance. Occasionally, when they encountered a headwind in a sound or straight too narrow to tack effectively, they used two pairs of oars and pulled the boat slowly but persistently towards their destination.

The two fishermen sat mostly quiet, following Kuhlin's orders, but otherwise doing nothing to be either of help or hindrance. Which was fair enough, Kuhlin thought. After all they had just lost command of their boat. He turned to Tapper, who huddled together with the fishermen in the small forward cabin while af Klint took over the tiller.

"Is there any chance of something hot to drink, bosun?"

Tapper shot a glance at the fishermen, silently relaying the question.

"There is some soup," the older fisherman said, pointing at the small one-stove galley. "You need to get that thing going though."

Tapper moved over to the stove. It was a small wood burning stove of cast iron, bolted to the deck of the fishing boat. It would do perfectly as long as the boat did not heel too much. If it did, he would have to hold the pot of soup straight or the liquid would all spill out.

"Yes, sir, I think I can produce some hot soup. But it'd be a lot easier if the boat would be on an even keel while I am heating it," he said to Kuhlin.

The commander nodded. "Very well. Get the stove going and then we will drop the sails and pull until you're done. After all, some exercise will do us good and help to keep us warm."

Captain Baker was worried. Not that he thought he couldn't complete this mission, he wouldn't have made post captain if he hadn't had a healthy portion of self-confidence. No, it was the subtle implications of this operation that worried him. As well as the weather. To start with the latter, the absolutely most important factor in any naval operation, it was increasingly less probable they would be able to sail into Norrköping itself. Even if the inlet was ice-free all the way in – which of course he had no way of knowing – the wind had veered into the west. It was still good enough for their current course and it would let them close the coast, albeit they would have to sail close-hauled. But getting inside the inlet was a completely different matter.

Norrköping was situated all the way in this inlet, Bråviken, which to Baker looked like a navigational nightmare. The very opening to the sea was wide enough, but littered with rocks and skerries, dangerous even in a favorable wind. But tacking through them? With a three masted square rigged vessel, a vessel in which the crew needed at least ten minutes to execute a complete tack? Well, nigh impossible. But that wasn't all either. A bit further in, Bråviken narrowed considerably, and Baker was certain that they would have the wind right into the nose in those very narrows.

He wondered how this place ever could have become a port. But then again, it wasn't a naval port and trading ships usually didn't tack. They just tucked themselves up in the lee of a nice island and waited for the wind to become right for the next passage. And if they had to wait a week, so be it.

But Baker didn't have a week. He needed to get into that town as quickly as possible – and then out again the same way. He could let her boats tow Tartar through the narrows of course. But that would be tedious and slow work and once in, there was the question of getting out again. He also had no idea about what coastal defenses were to be expected along the shores of the inlet. And who would be in charge of them.

Which led him to the second part of his worries. England and Sweden were supposed to be allies, but with a coup d'état on its way – or perhaps already completed – Baker couldn't be sure if his interference would be approved or at least tolerated. To be honest, he could not even know if he was about to get into trouble with his own admiralty. Post captains on foreign missions had a wide scope of initiative – but they were expected to take full responsibility for their actions, too.

And Baker's orders did, after all, only require him to observe. Of course, the orders were old, and things had happened since that could defend his taking action. The seizing of British ships on the west coast for example. But that had been ordered by the king, the very king he now was about to rescue. Not a good defense in a court-martial, he thought.

He was painfully aware that he mostly did this because he had become completely besotted with this woman. It was simply impossible to deny her anything. Which wasn't a good defense in a court-martial, either.

Baker pushed away the thought and returned to the nautical problems at hand. He could send boats with marines and a lieutenant into Norrköping while leaving Tartar anchored off the inlet. But this was a task that could not be delegated to a mere lieutenant. He would need to go himself and probably Anna as well. Hearing a rustling sound behind him, he turned in time to see Anna ascend the quarterdeck. She did not wear her cape and her face, arms and neck were flushed pink from the cold.

"Anna," he cried. "You need to get your cape. It's too cold up here, you will catch a fever."

Anna laughed. "You do not catch fevers from cold air, dear captain. But I won't stay long. In fact I came to lure you down into the cabin. I have something to discuss with you in private."

"Oh." Baker took a last look at the sails and rigging of his ship and followed her down towards the comparable warmth of the great cabin.

Winther got lucky at the second place. It was a miserable fishing village without even a decent tavern. Nor a decent harbour. A few rotten fishing boats were dragged into the reeds, or half sunk, filled with snow and ice. But the sea was only covered by ice to about twenty yards from the beach. Beyond that was open water. Dark gray water with the occasional whitecap.

There must have been some easterly storm recently that broke up the ice, there being virtually no offshore islands here, Winther contemplated. It was only a shame that it would have to be this utterly desolate place. He wondered where he was to stay. Should he just break into a barn or stable? If there even were any. Slowly he walked along the row of derelict houses, trying to get a glimpse through their windows without seeming too suspicious. Surely somebody must be home?

He stopped, sensing a motion behind a window.

"Hello there," he called. "Anyone at home?"

There was no answer.

"In the King's name, show yourself!" he tried.

There was some shuffling noise inside, then the window was thrust open and the face of an old weathered woman appeared.

"Take your king somewhere else," she croaked "It's the king who has taken my husband's life and this village's, too."

Winther groaned. "Listen, woman, I just need somewhere to stay for the night. I will pay you."

"I don't want the king's money nor you either," the woman replied. "I'm going to die here anyway. But try Maria, she'd need both money and a man. Last house in the row."

Things are starting to look up, Wither thought, walking towards the end of the road.

Chapter 17 – Trouble

Winther awoke with a smile, feeling the woman's warm body next to him. Maria was exactly what he needed to make this stay bearable. Having lost her husband in the war, she was still young enough to feel lonely at night and gladly accepted him and, of course, his money. She was a quiet woman, thin and weary, but warm and soft enough in places. Winther hugged her closer to himself under the thin blanket, hearing her sigh in her sleep.

He wondered how long he would need to stay here. His orders were clear enough, but all matters concerning the the Swedish navy were characterized by a great deal of insecurity, mess-ups and confusion. Especially during the winter, when all naval operations normally ceased.

As soon as first light trickled through the dirty glass of the window, he pushed Maria aside and rose from the bed.

"Are you leaving?" she asked sleepily.

"No. I will be back. Just going to get some fresh air."

The woman sighed and went back to sleep.

Winther left the house and walked the few yards to the beach. It was a gray morning and he felt some tension in the air. Perhaps there was a storm coming? At the moment it was still quiet though, the distant water almost placid. Then he realized that the wind came from the west, from the land, leaving the water undisturbed near the shore. He groaned when he came to the obvious conclusion. Until the wind shifted he would be stuck here. Might as well make the best of it, he thought and went back to the house.

"My dear captain," Anna said as softly as she could manage. "I am worried this is taking far too much time. We have been at sea two days now. Add the two days to get out of the ice, that makes four. For all we know, the king might be dead. The rebel troops can not be far from Stockholm and…"

Captain Baker took her in his arms. "Please, Anna. You will not get anywhere troubling yourself like this. The weather cannot be fought."

She sighed. "I know… I am just getting so concerned."

"It is very honorable of you, my dear. But surely there must be others who can save the king, or get him out of the country to safety?"

"I don't think so. Who would that be? I am the only one who has a powerful warship that isn't full of possible traitors."

Baker took her face between his hands and kissed her softly. "That you are."

Smiling at her he continued. "However, the wind does not look like shifting more easterly yet. Rather more to the south I'd reckon. That means we will close the coast today, but we will not get into Norrköping. You might consider going in yourself, or with a few of my marines, by boat and…"

Anna's body tensed, but she said nothing. Baker looked into her eyes. "Ah," he said. "I understand. You want the ship to be in plain sight of the city, white ensign aft and atop, guns run out and marines lining the railing?"

She smiled at him then. "That's the only way. The king would never come with me otherwise."

Tapper sat atop the fishing smack's cabin, looking out over the frothing water ahead. The wind had picked up, not enough to be of concern for a ship, but this wasn't a ship, and although seaworthy, their boat labored considerably in the chop. He turned and looked at the commander who stood in the stern, a wide grin on his face. Seeing the bosun, Kuhlin waved his hand.

"Don't worry, bosun, it's only a few more miles and we will be under the lee of the land when it curves southwards."

Tapper nodded. He knew this. It wasn't really the weather or the boat he was concerned about. It was Karin. For the first time ever he did not care about himself alone. During the whole of last summer's war in the Finnish archipelago he hadn't be overly worried or afraid of dying. But now it was different. He still thought about her almost every minute of his time awake, and dreamed about her frequently when asleep. And while this felt utterly amazing, it also made him more aware of the dangers his life entailed.

"Bosun Tapper!" Kuhlin called.

"Aye, yes, sir?"

"Take the tiller for a while?"

"Of course, sir." Tapper made his way aft. Taking over the tiller he saw that Kuhlin was smiling at him.

"Sorry, sir?" he blushed.

"Still in love, are you, bosun?" Kuhlin chuckled.

"Well, yes, sir, I guess. Why do you ask?"

Kuhlin laughed. "I called you back here twice before you even heard me, bosun. You'd better pull yourself together in case there is some action further ahead."

Tapper swallowed. "Of course, sir."

Further north, on the Åland sea, the ice was still solid. And two weeks into the month of March, the

Russian attack on Åland began. General Döbeln had prepared his defense best he could, considering the circumstances. He had also, perhaps slightly in defiance of his orders, prepared a line of retreat. Or it had been anticipation. Because, when the Russians came, so came new orders. Orders, not signed by the king – who never would have given up Åland without a fight – but by those who had removed him from his powers.

Döbeln, who was loyal to the king, was both furious and relieved. Furious, because he had not been able, or allowed, to prevent the king from being overthrown. Relieved though, because he now could evacuate these islands and probably save thousands of lives in the process.

Thus, without any more serious bloodshed than the occasional skirmish ever happening on Åland, the Swedish army retreated over the ice towards the mainland, and the town of Grisslehamn. Thanks to a great deal of subterfuge on Döbelns part, the Russians were led to believe the Swedish army would stay, negotiate and finally surrender, giving Döbeln the necessary time to get most of his equipment off Åland without even having to fight a proper rear-guard action.

However, the Russians had their own orders. To bring this war to an end quickly and conclusively they advanced themselves, following the Swedish army over the ice once again, towards the Swedish mainland itself. Döbeln, using deceit rather than force, however, succeeded to prevent them from getting ashore. Fearing the ice breaking up, the Russians went back to Åland in the end, exactly as they did much further north, where another trek over the ice proved similarly unsuccessful.

Only in the far North, Russian troops managed to actually get their feet on Swedish soil, and there they stayed until the war eventually ended more than six months later.

Chapter 18 – Camilla

For two more days Winther repeated his daily routine. He walked along the beach, looking out over the sea to the East, looking up into the sky, judging the wind and weather, feeling quite at a loss. After all, he was a soldier, not a sailor and what did he know about things nautical – or meteorological.

The evenings and nights he spent with Maria, savoring her warmth and affection. He knew that this was utterly temporary, and so did she. Still they lived together almost like a couple, giving each other the kind of imaginary security people only seem to appreciate during times of war or extreme personal distress.

Every morning, at first light, he left the cottage, went down to the beach, trying to penetrate the grayness in search for what he so wanted to see. Because it would be the end of this desperate mission. On the other hand, he did not want it to happen, imagining an eternal bubble of bliss, living here, with Maria, and forgetting loyalties, wars and politics completely.

The third morning, though, when he went down to the sea, he felt the change directly. The wind blew in his face, from the southwest instead of west, and it wasn't even cold. The sky wasn't blue by all means, but it wasn't the dense grayness of the last days either. And about 200 yards off the edge of the ice, lay a ship at anchor. It was one of the Swedish navy's proudest vessels, not at all the biggest, but one of the most well kept and widely used. Drawn by Fredrik Henrik af Chapman, the same man who invented the gunboats Kuhlin and his men had served on during the last summer, Camilla was of a design especially adapted for the Baltic sea. Carrying forty 24-pounders, she was as heavily armed as any comparable frigate of her time, but Chapman had given her much finer lines and a shallower draft than anything else afloat of that size – less than ten feet. This he achieved by allowing much less room for storage and provisions, the frigates of the Bellona class not at all intended to roam the oceans of the world. In fact, Camilla had never been farther than the Mediterranean, while escorting merchantmen and fighting Barbary pirates.

There were other things that made her special as well. Her great cabin for one, was situated below the quarterdeck, like on an East Indiaman. Thus, she could carry an extra main battery gun port on each side, as well as proper stern ports, a great advantage if attacked by gunboats in a calm.

Sub-lieutenant Winther, of course, had no idea

about all of this. Still, even being a soldier, he could appreciate beauty when he saw it. Camilla rode high, having been ordered to sea out of her winter sleep far too early there hadn't been time to provision her completely. Her rigging was all newly tarred and the hull freshly painted, despite the lack of resources at the main navy yard at Carlskrona.

Still, Winther could admire what he saw. He was amazed by the contrast of man-made wooden beauty against the gloomy winter sky. The white sails, prettily furled, the gleaming black of the Stockholm tar and the gilded paint of the hull. While he stood there, gaping at the sight, he realized that a boat had been on its way towards him for quite a while. He straightened up and started to walk back to the cottage in order to retrieve his dispatches.

When he returned, the boat had reached the edge of the ice. Winther walked awkwardly towards the waiting men. A very young looking midshipman greeted him and helped him into the boat. As soon as he was seated in the stern sheets, the boat's crew lowered their oars and started to pull. Winther felt cold immediately. Out on the water, the wind was much more tangible, penetrating his clothes and making him shiver. But the pull to the ship did not take long and soon Winther faced his next obstacle.

The hull of the frigate towered above him like a

castle. The gun ports were all closed black squares against bright yellow paint. And the entry port, two decks above him seemed as far away as an unreachable bird perched high up in a tree. There was some sort of wooden steps extending out of the hull, and rope handrails on either side of them, but it all looked awfully unstable. Not to speak of the fact that in order to get to the lowest step he would have to almost jump onto it from the boat – and the boat was bobbing around all the time.

The young midshipman, sensing Winther's unease, smiled at him and, judging the right moment expertly, gave him a healthy shove, yelling: "Off you go!" Winther jumped, gripped the ropes for dear life and found himself clambering up the side of the ship like a monkey. Still, he made it all right, and found himself, gasping, in front of an older officer right inside the entry port.

"Welcome aboard Camilla," the lieutenant said.

Winther, clasping his dispatch bag, tried to smile. "Thank you, sir."

"If you have regained yourself, I will take you to the captain," the lieutenant continued, a smirk on his face.

Anna slept uneasily, dreaming weird dreams about sleigh rides, storms and fierce rebel troops chasing her through a forest. It did not help either, that Captain Baker left her several times during the night in order to check Tartar's moorings. The wind was shifting and increasing, and the small island that had sheltered them no longer did so. Still, Baker wanted to wait for first light before he had the frigate moved. When he finally ordered all hands on deck to unmoor ship, Anna rose as well, put her furry cape around her and went on deck.

The weather did look a lot nicer, but it did not feel it, what with the wind being stronger and more chilly and the water having become more choppy and restless. She sighed. Hopefully the wind was blowing from a direction now which enabled them to get into this cursed inlet. She was quite near despairing, that much she could admit. Most probably everything was over already and all her efforts were of no use whatsoever. A pleasure cruise on her own frigate, that was what this probably was by now. The thought still made her smile. She had never been on a pleasure cruise before.

She looked out over the water, her thoughts wandering to Eric and their time together at his estate. That had been special. She sighed, trying to pull herself together. Whatever her feelings for him, she knew now that she never could live like that. Well, perhaps for a while longer, or for extended periods of time even. But not for the rest of her life. She turned around, looking over the quarterdeck. Captain Baker stood next to the big wheel, giving orders to his first lieutenant. Anna liked the Englishman, she decided. Not only because he had power and commanded a ship, but also because he seemed to care about her in an unselfish manner she hadn't met in so many men before. In Eric, yes, he was the same. But would he really risk his career for her, like Baker apparently did without even thinking about it? Probably not. She wondered why he did it. Sometimes she really did not understand men at all.

Aboard the fishing smack conditions were deteriorating. The wind chill made the men cold to the bone, the warm soup was gone and the small cabin did not provide more than temporary shelter. While the wind still wasn't too strong for the boat to be sailed, it had shifted enough to force them to tack into it, increasing the apparent wind speed and thus the chill. To sail the boat, two men were needed on deck at the same time, while the rest huddled together in the cabin. Kuhlin, who did not stand a watch himself, was permanently occupied with navigation. They only had a primitive chart of the area and he was very much depending on visual observation of the water and the surrounding islands. Fortunately the boat had a very shallow draft, so shoals could often be seen before they hit them. Still, they touched rock several times, bringing frightened expressions to the two fishermen's faces.

"Sir?" Tapper touched Kuhlin's sleeve carefully.

"Yes, bosun?"

"May I suggest we take ashore somewhere and rest, sir? I think we are all getting pretty exhausted... And..."

"I know, bosun." Kuhlin sighed. The first night they had been sailing through without stopping, three men at a time trying to get some sleep on the wooden berths in the small cabin. They all knew that time was of the essence what with the frigate sailing so much faster. But Tapper was right. They were no use to anyone if they lost too much of their strength. He looked at the chart.

"Alright, bosun, we will put ashore and rest for four hours. We might even get a fire going."

Tapper smiled wearily. "Thank you, sir."

Winther entered Camilla's great cabin with careful steps, clutching the dispatch bag. He hadn't thought a ship could feel so big. All he had been on before were open boats or ferries, a gunboat even. But this was like a house, actually much bigger than the cottage Maria lived in. In the middle of the cabin stood a wooden desk, and in front of it was a man, wearing a full captain's uniform.

"Ah, Sub-Lieutenant Winther?"

"Yes, sir." Winther stood to attention.

"At ease, soldier," the captain said, smiling. "This isn't the army. My name is Trolle, by the way. Please take a seat. Do you want a glass of something? Actually, I even have some wine... Got it from a Danish brig we took on our way here. You have orders for me I trust?"

Winther handed the dispatch bag to the captain, then sat down on a chair next to the desk. Trolle opened the bag and produced a sealed envelope. Putting the bag on the desk he carefully examined the seal. Then he looked at Winther.

"Did you say you wanted some wine?"

Winther nodded.

Captain Trolle called to his servant and ordered two glasses of wine. He sat down behind the desk, holding the envelope into his hands.

"Do you know what these dispatches say, Winther?" he asked.

Winther cleared his throat. "Not exactly, sir."

Trolle raised an eyebrow. "What does that mean, sub-lieutenant - not exactly?"

"Well, sir; I know what it says about the political situation in Stockholm. But I don't know what your orders are."

"Ah." Trolle nodded. "Let's see then." He broke the seal, pulled out several sheets of paper and started to read.

The wine came and both men raised their glasses for a toast. Suddenly Trolle laughed. "So, sub-lieutenant, whom are we to toast, do you think?"

Winther looked bewildered into his glass. It was usual to toast the king on those occasions, but perhaps there already wasn't a king anymore. Or at least not the same.

"I don't know," he said quietly.

"I hear the British have this toast they use in their gunrooms..." Trolle said, still chuckling. Raising his glass he continued: "To wives and sweethearts – may they never meet."

Chapter 19 – Confrontation

Captain Baker looked at the rigging of HMS Tartar, observing every detail and finding nothing to complain about. It was time. "Mr. Reeman," he called. "Weigh anchor if you please."

"Aye, aye, sir," Reeman replied and walked forward. The bosun's pipe started to shrill, sending men running to their stations for weighing anchor. The big capstan was manned and on the given order, the men started to walk, leaning their bodies against the bars, turning the big drum slowly. Inch by inch the dripping wet anchor cable was hauled inboard, slowly first, then a little faster as the ship gained momentum.

"Up and down!" A man called from the bows. He was leaning over the side of the ship, observing the anchor cable which now pointed straight down into the water. Then: "Anchor aweigh!"

"Hoist inner and outer jib, prepare to let fall topsails," Baker ordered.

On the bowsprit two white triangular sails rose, filled with wind and started to push the bows of the frigate around. As she slowly began to point northwest, Baker ordered the topsails to be let fall and sheeted in. The ship was under way.

MISS ANNA'S FRIGATE

On the poop, the after-most end of the ship's deck, Anna leaned against the rail, watching the spectacle. When they had first left Dalarö she had been below, mostly because of the cold, but also from exhaustion after the arduous work of getting the ship through the ice, and perhaps a little sore after having gotten Baker to do it in the first place. She smiled. The captain had been a bit of a surprise in that respect, letting her find some undisclosed desires he probably didn't even know he had.

But now she reveled in the sight. There was something magical over how this big a contraption could be moved by the wind alone, silently and gracefully, yet so powerful a vessel. She thought of the 32 heavy guns on the main deck and wondered if they would need to use them. She had witnessed big guns being fired before of course, last summer during the gunboat campaign. But that had been single guns on small boats. Powerful enough, to be sure, but Baker had explained to her that on a frigate, all guns on one side could be fired simultaneously, that in fact this was how it was done regularly, at least in the beginning of a battle. Anna tried to imagine the sound, the smell of gunpowder and the smoke, enveloping everything, making eyes tear and breathing hard.

As the ship settled on a steady course to the

Northwest, Baker ordered extra lookouts to be posted in the bows.

"Let them watch the water close ahead for signs of rocks or shoals, Mr. Reeman. Also, keep sounding the depth continuously. Oh, and please send word for the master."

The sailing master, Pope, arrived shortly, a rolled chart tucked under his arm.

"Ah, Mr. Pope," Baker said. "Now, what do you make of these waters?"

"They are evil, frankly, sir," Pope replied, wiping his forehead with his free hand, sweating, despite the cold. "I really would want to have a pilot aboard, sir."

"A pilot, eh? In the middle of a war? Rubbish. We will have to do our own piloting, Mr. Pope. As we have done many times before."

"Of course, sir." Pope unrolled the chart and put it on the railing between the quarterdeck and the waist of the ship, holding it spread out with his hands.

"Now, as you can see, there are, well... There is an uncountable number of islands and skerries. However, there seem to be two channels that might be usable, sir."

Baker nodded, studying the chart. "Do you think they might be marked?"

"I have no idea. I would not expect them to be

marked by buoys, like they would be at home, but there might be some signs painted on rocks or the like, sir."

Baker grunted. He had seen those markings before, in the Finnish archipelago. They were almost never shown on the chart and their value was doubtful in the least. Unless one had a pilot who knew the waters.

Hearing the rustling of skirts, he turned around and smiled at Anna who had left her place at the aft railing in order to join the men. Anna, returning his smile, put her hand softly on his arm. "Have you found a way to sail us into Norrköping at last?"

"I trust so," Baker replied. "At least the wind is right for it and there are two channels which should be deep enough."

Anna took a look at the chart. "How far is it, then?"

"Mr. Pope?" Baker relayed the question.

"We could be there before dark. If the wind holds, if there is no ice in the inlet and if..."

Baker laughed. "Come, Mr. Pope, don't sound so despairing. At least there are no tides."

"I wish there were..." the sailing master muttered into his beard.

Commander Kuhlin stood on the beach of the small

island, stretching his frozen limbs. They had extended their rest to a full eight hours after finally having put ashore, gathered firewood and, with the help of some oil from the boat, got the cold and damp wood to burn. They had even caught some fish, or the fishermen had, miraculously, during the last hours of daylight. Fed and comparatively warm, they had fallen asleep instantly.

At first light, however, the fire had been out for several hours and they were once again cold to the bone. Kuhlin walked along the beach in order to get warm. This was really a desperate mission, he thought. At least last time they rescued Anna it had been summer. He and af Klint had used a fishing smack as well then, quite similar this one in fact. But then they had sneaked into a town, not tried to keep pace with a frigate at sea. Kuhlin frowned. Even if they could keep up and find the British frigate in the end, what were they supposed to do? How were they supposed to persuade Anna to abandon her mission and come with them? How were they even to stop a British frigate, or signal to her that they want to talk to the passenger – or the captain?

Kuhlin turned back towards the camp when a blur on the horizon caught his eye. "Tapper!" he shouted. "My glass – quickly!"

The bosun appeared, still sleepy-looking, and

handed him the telescope. Kuhlin extended it and raised it to his eye, slowly sweeping the horizon.

"Sir?" Tapper asked curiously.

"A ship, Tapper," Kuhlin replied. "I think it's a frigate."

"Our friend the Englishman?"

Kuhlin put down the glass and shook his head. "I don't think so, bosun. She seems to have too many gunports... Have a look yourself." He handed Tapper the telescope.

The bosun raised it carefully. "Where away, sir?"

Kuhlin pointed with his arm.

"Ah, got her..."

"What do you make of her, bosun?"

"Wait a second, sir... You're right, it's not Tartar, she's supposed to be a 32, yes?"

"Aye."

"This one has 19 gunports... Doesn't she? A 38?"

"That was what I thought as well," Kuhlin said. "Great. Two frigates around. In the middle of the winter..."

"Sir, there's something odd about her quarterdeck... Looks a little like a merchantman..."

"A merchantman? With all those guns?"

"No, not a merchantman, just looks like one... You know, with the great cabin like... Misplaced..."

"Like on Bellona?" Kuhlin exclaimed.

171

"Yes! Or Camilla! It's a Chapman frigate, sir: I'm sure of it." He put the glass down and gave it back to Kuhlin who immediately raised it again and studied the ship.

"You might be right, bosun. But what is she doing here? They are all supposed to be laid up in Carlskrona over the winter."

"There's only one reasonable answer," af Klint said. He had been sneaking up on the pair and was now standing beside them.

"Ah, Eric," Kuhlin smiled. "And that answer would be?"

"To stop Tartar. Or get the king themselves."

Kuhlin nodded. "Perhaps. But that would imply the king is no longer in charge. How would the captain of that frigate be able to know that. And whose orders would he be following?"

"In any case, I think we need to get going," Eric pointed out.

"You're right. Let's get under way."

Camilla was creaming along under full plain sail, precariously close to skerries and rocks much smaller ships would be weary of. But the frigate was built for this, and her captain had sailed these waters all his life. He also was in a hurry. It was absolutely essential to reach the narrows first. Once past them, there was too much open water and too many people in sight of what could occur. Not that Trolle really thought there was any risk of a serious confrontation. He had met the Englishman during the blockade of Estonia last summer and he had seemed to him like a typical English gentleman. Polite, pleasant and eager to do his duty. The question now was why he regarded this mission as his duty in the first place. Baker had no official orders. Britain had not offered any help to the overthrown king either. On the contrary, after his seizing the British merchant ships on the West coast, one would expect them to be happy with a new Swedish government.

This had all thoroughly been discussed in his dispatches. Not that Trolle cared. Like most Swedish naval officers he hated politics. This coup d'état business was entirely an army thing, what with generals and field marshals always being so deeply involved in politics. Still, he had his orders and would carry them out – of course. And he had the perfect vessel for it. Camilla was better suited for close quarter navigation in shallow waters. She even carried more guns than Tartar, 40 against 32, even though two of his guns were mounted in the stern. On the other hand, the English ship might be a tad faster with his own not being copper coated and probably slowed down by marine growth on the bottom. Also the British were darned good at fighting. There were numerous stories of far inferior British ships having taken much stronger enemies in close battle at sea.

Of course, there could never be a real battle, could there? The two nations were still officially allies after all. And Baker must finally realize that his mission did not have official support?

He turned to Sub-lieutenant Winther who stood at the leeward railing, slightly green in his face.

"Are you not well, soldier?" Trolle chuckled. This served the boy right, he thought. There was something with the officer he did not like. It was hard to put a finger on it really, perhaps it was only because he wasn't navy. One could never really trust these mud-and-forest people. Too many places to hide, too many distractions from duty – too much politics in their ranks.

"I'm all right, sir, thank you, sir," Winther managed before he spun around, leaned over the rail and retched.

"Sail ho!" the outlook cried from the masthead. HMS Tartar was still on a northwesterly course between the islands off the mouth of Bråviken. They had entered the Southern channel and passed through it about halfway. It had been an interesting exercise in piloting, with the channel being very narrow in parts between a bigger island and the mainland. Fortunately there had been some markers, whose purpose they had been able to guess correctly. Now, the channel turned more northerly and leaving the big island to their right behind, a stretch of comparatively open water emerged ahead. And on the far side of this stretch of water, against the Northern shore of the inlet, there was a ship.

"Ship on the starboard bow!" the lookout cried.

"What kind of ship?" Captain Baker demanded.

"Looks like a frigate, sir!"

"Mr. Reeman, take a glass aloft and have a look, if you please."

"Aye, aye, sir." The first lieutenant started to climb the mizzen shrouds, telescope slung across his back like an archer's quiver. A moment later he was on the mizzen fighting top, telescope raised.

"Deck there," he called.

"Go ahead!"

"It's a frigate, sir, alright. Looks like one of the Swedish ones we met off Estonia."

Baker grunted. What was a Swedish frigate doing here? "What's her course?"

"Converging, sir. She seems to be inbound like us, but through the northern channel."

Baker felt a hand on his arm. Anna. He turned towards her, concern on his face.

"A Swedish frigate?" she asked.

"Yes. There is really only one reason for her to be here, you know..."

"Two, in fact my dear captain. To get the king themselves, or to stop me from doing it."

Baker smiled. "Yes. But that's really one and the same isn't it?"

"Perhaps." Anna narrowed her eyes. "What are you going to do about this frigate?"

"That depends on what she is going to do about us, doesn't it?" Baker looked towards the distant vessel. Then he made up his mind.

"There's no reason not to expect the worst, however," he said. "Mr. Reeman! Come down if you please."

With the first officer standing on deck once again, Baker took at deep breath. Exhaling slowly, he turned his gaze on the lieutenant. "Well, Mr. Reeman, if you'd be so kind as to have the ship cleared for action."

Bosun's pipes shrilled and the ship came alive with men running to their stations, tearing down canvas walls in the great and officer's cabins and carrying furniture and carpets into the hold below. Others were wetting and sanding the deck in order to make it less prone to catch fire and less slippery in case of extensive bloodshed. Ship's boys were hauling canvas cartridges filled with gunpowder on deck and gun crews were stacking cannon balls and grape shot next to their guns.

Aloft, spars were secured with chains in order to not have them fall on deck if shot away. Marines in red coats loaded and primed their muskets, waiting to be deployed in the fighting tops and along the railing.

"We'll have the marines out of the way, for now," Baker told his first lieutenant. "Don't want to look too eager to fight, do we?" He grinned. They also would not open the gun ports or show any other apparent sign of being cleared for action. After all, Britain wasn't at war with Sweden.

Chapter 20 – Consequences

Commander Kuhlin stared towards the hazy horizon. Well, it wasn't really the horizon, it was just the visibility being limited to only a few miles. He swore. So long as it doesn't start snowing, he thought. Then they would have no chance of finding the frigate. They barely had any now.

"What are we going to do?" Eric af Klint asked, stepping up besides him.

Kuhlin sighed. "In this weather, there's really only one thing we can do. Carry on as before and hope that frigate hasn't anything to do with this."

"Do you really think she might not?"

"No. I think she's after the Tartar. Or Anna."

Eric swallowed. "How could they know about her plans?"

"It's not really necessary for them to know. The fact that she's missing and the Tartar has sailed might be enough to look for them…"

Erik frowned. "It doesn't really matter, does it? There's nothing else we can do, except continue."

Kuhlin nodded. "If only this haze would lift."

They sailed on. Shortly after noon the haze did lift, at least partly, as a bleak sun burned away the moisture in the air. They changed course to the

Southwest, following the Northern shore of Bråviken. As soon as they were past the last two islands on their starboard side they would have a much better view of the narrows. And hopefully, one or two frigates would be there.

Bosun Tapper stood in the bows of the fishing smack, keeping lookout to starboard, watching the first of the two islands draw closer, when he heard a distant rumbling sound.

"Did you hear that?" he shouted aft.

"Aye," af Klint replied. "Gunfire."

Kuhlin opened his mouth to say something when there was another rumble. He swore.

Captain Baker couldn't believe it. Not only had Camilla signaled them to heave-to for the captain to repair aboard, but upon his slight hesitation she even had fired a gun to emphasize her point. A signal gun, not loaded thank God, but a gun nonetheless.

"I can't believe it. The impertinent dog," he said to Anna who stood next to him comforting him with a small hand on his arm. "No-one orders a British warship to heave-to. It's just not done."

He looked at his first officer, who stood crestfallen, looking at the Swedish frigate, about two cables away on their starboard bow, slowly moving under topsails alone, across their course.

"Do not stand there like a sheep," Baker told him. "Hold that course of yours and be prepared to follow my orders quickly and efficiently."

Reeman straightened his back. "Aye aye, sir."

"What are you going to do?" Anna asked, her hand on the captain's arm tightening its grip.

Baker smiled at her, but the smile did not reach his eyes. "Stand on. Whatever the circumstances, a British ship cannot be subdued."

A minute passed. Then smoke erupted from Camilla's forecastle again, another bang, and this time there was a spout of water twenty yards in front of HMS Tartar's bows.

"The devil take you, Trolle," Baker muttered. Loudly he said: "Keep going, Mr. Reeman."

He judged the distance to the Swedish frigate. She was still one and a half cables away. At this speed that would give him only a few minutes until the ships would collide, if neither of them altered course or speed. Baker studied Camilla. Her gun ports were still closed, except the most forward one, from which the shot across their bows had come.

What would Trolle do? How far was he prepared to go? Would he really risk a fight? Baker made his decision.

"Mr. Reeman, run out the guns, if you please."

"Aye aye, sir!"

In unison Tartar's gun ports were flung open, and men hauled the heavy ropes that pulled the guns outwards, muzzles extending, the frigate baring her teeth like an angry animal.

Only seconds later, the same thing happened aboard Camilla. Anna gasped, clasping Baker's arm firmly. Baker put his other hand on hers.

"I think it might perhaps be better if you went below, my dear."

Anna frowned. "And miss the action? Oh no, I will stay right here."

Baker sighed. "Very well. But if there is firing try to keep your head low."

She nodded and smiled at him. Not that he'd believed she would. But one had to try, he thought. Turning his attention back to the Swedish frigate he narrowed his eyes.

"She's falling off," the sailing master cried.

"One point to larboard," Baker ordered.

Camilla had changed her course first, slightly to starboard, towards the land. Baker took this as a good sign. At least Trolle didn't want to actually lay her alongside. So as a sign of good will, if that was at all possible what with both ships cleared for action and guns run out, he had slightly changed course away from the Swedish frigate – and also, unfortunately from his intended course. Both ships were now sailing on a parallel course at about a cable's distance. Tartar had the weather gauge, meaning she was on the windward side of Camilla, giving her more options of maneuvering than the Swede. In a battle in open waters, this would have been an immense advantage, but here, amongst islands and shallows it wasn't necessarily the case.

"What is he going to do?" Anna asked.

Baker shrugged. "I have no idea. I still doubt he will open fire in earnest."

Aboard Camilla, Sub-lieutenant Winther stared at the British frigate. He was frightened. The ship was so near, and the guns were so big, bigger than anything he had ever seen. Being a soldier, he was used to field artillery, thin tiny barrels on carriages with huge wheels, firing cannonballs smaller than an egg, weighing six pounds perhaps eight. These monsters weighed almost a ton and the cannonballs were four times as heavy as those on land. He didn't want to even imagine what their effect would be. They would go right through the thick planking of the ship, splintering it, sending hundreds of sharp fragments into the air and bodies of the unprotected men. He shuddered.

On the quarterdeck, captain Trolle stood with a

smile on his face. He had known Baker to be a stubborn bastard. The English had this thing with ruling the waves and never giving in to anyone else's orders. Still, he would stop him, one way or the other. He called up a mental picture of the chart of the inlet. The Northern part, where they were sailing now, was deep and safe enough. But a little further to the South was an area of interesting shallows and partly submerged rocks.

"Two points to larboard," he ordered.

"She is altering course," The first lieutenant remarked.

"I can see that, thank you, Mr. Reeman. We will do the same, I think. Keep her on a parallel course at all times, if you please."

"Aye aye, sir."

Baker wondered what Trolle would do next. Clearly he wasn't too keen on an exchange of broadsides. Which was good. But it also made it more difficult to plan his own moves. He could not just fight his way through, like he would have done if his opponent had been, well, French or something.

"How are you coping, soldier?" Trolle called to Sub-lieutenant Winther. "You look a bit pale, do you not? Are you well?"

Winther tried to smile. "I'm alright, sir. Just not used to the sea!" He hesitated. "By your leave, sir, what are you going to do? I mean, how are we to stop her? Do we really have to fight her?"

Trolle chuckled. "That depends on what you mean by fight. I don't plan to sink her, you know. But there might be needed a certain amount of force, I am afraid. These English are very stubborn creatures."

He strolled to the larboard side of the deck. Holding a mizzen shroud for support, he leaned over the side and looked ahead. Then his gaze wandered towards the British frigate, sailing on a parallel course still, about half a ship's length behind.

"I think it is time," he said to himself, then raised his voice. "Prepare to come about!"

"What's he doing now?" Anna asked, her eyes on the Swedish frigate. On Camilla's deck, men swarmed, seemingly without purpose, but then order returned and the big vessel started to change course once again, more radically this time, not only the rudder being turned to another angle, but also the yards that hold the sails.

"She's coming about," Baker explained. "Turning through the wind so as to pass directly under our stern. And as she is ahead of us, it will be very close."

"Is that dangerous?"

"In a normal battle, yes. Very dangerous. He could rake us, shoot cannonballs right through our stern windows. They would fly all the way through the ship, there being no wooden bulkheads to stop them."

Anna gasped.

"But I don't think he will do that now. This is just a game of cat and mouse I would suspect."

"But surely..." Anna hesitated.

"Don't worry, my dear, I've some aces of my own," Baker smiled. "Mr. Reeman, would you be so kind as to clew up the topsails for a minute?"

As the hands pulled on the clew lines, the lower corners of the sails rose, lessening the sail area and slowing down the ship. The Camilla, supposed to pass closely under Tartar's stern was now pointing directly at her quarterdeck.

"She is going to ram us!" Anna exclaimed.

"Oh no," Baker replied calmly, "She isn't. Look!"

Camilla started to turn again, more to larboard, further away from the wind. Like birds in a mating dance, Anna thought, as the other frigate performed a complete turn, presenting her stern gallery, then the other side, until the two ships sailed on a parallel course again, but now with Camilla half a ship's length behind the Englishman.

Captain Baker laughed. "That was fun," he said, chuckling. Anna, smiling wearily, didn't really think so. This wasn't helping her to get the king out, and frankly, she was starting to despair.

"I am sorry to interrupt your... Eh... Amusement, but I really think we should hurry and..."

"Wait!" Baker said, looking at the Swedish frigate, which was altering her course again, but this time in the wrong direction. "Down!" he shoved Anna hard behind the binnacle, making her yelp in surprise. At the same instant, Camilla's broadside erupted in smoke and fire.

Chapter 21 - Survival

The broadside took Baker completely by surprise. He stood, his mouth agape, as the cannonballs whined through the rigging of his ship, holes appearing in her sails, cordage ripping, wood splintering and men in the fighting tops screaming in agony. One sailor fell as the yard he was working on was ripped in two, landing on the deck with a soft thud, not to move ever again.

Baker shook his head. This wasn't happening. He looked around him. Anna was crouching behind the binnacle, unhurt thank God. In fact, the decks were undamaged, the broadside apparently having been aimed high in order to damage the rigging. Like the French, Baker thought distastefully. He looked towards the Swedish frigate which now had resumed her original course as if nothing had happened.

"Sir?" Mr. Reeman looked at his captain, eyebrows raised.

"Of course, Mr. Reeman. Be so kind as to return fire."

"Two points to starboard!" Reeman roared. "Aim low."

Slowly, Tartar turned to starboard and one after another the gun captains raised their hands, fist clenched, as Camilla appeared in their view. As the last gun was thus reported ready, Reeman looked at Baker, who nodded.

"Fire!" Reeman ordered. And Tartar's broadside erupted, belching hot smoke, fire and iron. Anna gasped, her hands tightly pressed over her ears. Then she looked at the other ship. It was difficult to see the effect of their broadside. Baker had aimed low, as was the British way, in order to damage the hull and kill people, not damage the sails and clip the enemy's wings. But the hull was the most solid part of the ship and while there were some parts of the railing clearly missing, Camilla looked exactly as she had before.

"Did we do any damage at all?" Anna asked, eyes wide.

Aboard Camilla, Captain Trolle examined the damage the broadside had done to his ship. One gun had been turned over, rendering it useless and badly maiming the men who happened to end up under the heavy iron. Other men were injured by splinters, most of them lightly. But only a few yards from him lay Sub-lieutenant Winther, sans his head, blood still trickling out of his neck.

Trolle sighed and turned back to the task at hand. Baker had reacted as expected, of course. Perhaps firing on him hadn't been the best move, but after the failed maneuver he needed a way to distract Baker and, preferably, cripple his ship.

"We will try again," he told his first lieutenant. "Prepare to come about, and warn the starboard gun crews. It will be their turn next."

"She's turning again," Reeman observed as Camilla's foresails started to flap.

"Yes," Baker replied. "And this time she even might succeed. As she is behind us, we cannot block her by slowing down."

"We could alter course to starboard and give her our broadside as she turns?"

"We could," Baker grunted. "But we would then lose the weather gauge, for what that's worth in these waters. Still, we will do no such thing, we will come about as well and meet her on the same tack."

And Tartar started to turn southwards as well.

"What now, Mr. Pope?" Baker narrowed his eyes at the sailing master who had come running from below, where he probably had been hiding under his charts, Baker thought.

"Captain, sir, on this course, there are shallows ahead. I am not sure we will pass over, sir." Pope was sweating heavily.

"Calm down, Mr. Pope. Our Swedish friend is on

the same course, is he not? Surely he must know his waters?"

"But, sir, the Admiralty charts..."

"Sod the Admiralty, Mr. Pope. I am certain, the Swedes have perfectly reliable charts over their own waters. That captain over there, Trolle, he is no fool. He has sailed these waters all of his life. So I suggest you just go back down to your charts and correct them."

"But, sir..."

"Dismissed, Mr. Pope," Baker hissed, turning his gaze back to the Swedish frigate just in time to see her broadside erupt in smoke once again.

"Fire," he shouted and as the Swedish cannonballs once again whined through the rigging and showered the men on deck in splinters, broken cordage and blocks, their own guns boomed their reply.

Anna stood at the binnacle, eyes wide, too stunned to move when she heard someone shout a warning. Looking up, she saw the big mizzen boom bulge and splinter, the aft end toppling down towards the deck and her. She threw herself out of the way, ending up at the lee bulwarks, staggered against them for support. There was a bit of the railing missing, but she caught a grip on the wood next to the hole and pulled herself up slowly. Just as she began to look around her, a shudder went through the ship, wood creaked and then it came to a sudden stop, flinging everything forward, breaking spars as the masts strained against already half-broken shrouds and stays, and Anna was cast off her feet again, finding no support now, tumbling through the hole in the bulwarks and into the sea.

"Cease fire," Captain Trolle ordered. "Secure guns, and close gun ports." The battle was over, his goal achieved. Best not to give Baker an excuse for more bloodshed. Sure, there was a risk the Englishman would continue to fire as Camilla slowly passed, but Trolle didn't expect it. Baker, after all, was a gentleman and would accept his defeat.

"Prepare to dip the ensign," he ordered.

Gracefully, Camilla drew past the British frigate, passing over the very shallows that had stopped Tartar dead in her tracks, with several feet of water to spare. When she was level with the other ship's quarterdeck, the big Swedish flag flying from the mizzen gaff boom was slowly lowered half way down in greeting. As a bewildered looking midshipman scurried aft aboard Tartar and did the same, Camilla's ensign rose to the top again. Slowly, she sailed past and disappeared between the islands, carefully threading her way back to the main channel towards Norrköping.

"Good God," af Klint exclaimed as the fishing smack finally made it past the islands and they had a clear view ahead. There was HMS Tartar, sitting at an odd angle, bows too high, fore-topmast hanging in its shrouds over the starboard bow, mizzen boom splintered, shortly, she was a complete mess. Her gun ports were still open, her guns still run out, but yet she did not look menacing any longer. Men were working on her, cutting away broken cordage, clearing the decks of tattered sails.

Kuhlin steered the boat towards the frigate, while Tapper and af Klint stood in her bows, frantically trying to get a glimpse of Anna on the ship's deck. But she was not to be seen, not even as the boat sailed closer and hove-to under the stern of the frigate.

"Ahoy, Tartar," Kuhlin called.

A young officer appeared, looking down at them a worried expression on his face.

"Do you need any assistance?" Kuhlin asked.

The officer shook his head, but there was a look of uncertainty in his eyes.

"Can I speak to your captain? I am an acquaintance of his, my name is Kuhlin. Commander Kuhlin?"

"I'm sorry, sir, the captain is... Indisposed. And we are aground and have been fired on by one of your ships and..."

Clearly that officer was in a state of shock, Kuhlin thought. "Are you in command, then? Do you know anything about your passenger, Miss Anna?"

The English officer looked startled.

"I don't know... I mean, yes, I'm in command, I am the first officer..."

"Is Miss Anna alright?"

"I don't know, I haven't seen her since we ran aground."

"Christ!" af Klint exclaimed.

Kuhlin took a deep breath trying to keep calm.

"Could you send someone to look for her, please? Or let us aboard?"

The officer hesitated. "I will send someone to look for her. Can't let you aboard, we are... Um... In a bit of a mess here."

So they waited, impatiently, nervously. Eric af Klint was nearing a state of despair, when the officer came back to the railing, shaking his head. "She seems not to be aboard any more," he said.

Eric groaned. Sitting down on a thwart, he took his head between his hands.

"She must have gone overboard with the impact," bosun Tapper observed in a low voice.

"We will conduct a search," Kuhlin said. Raising his voice he addressed the English officer. "Can you spare a boat's crew to look for her, lieutenant?"

Reeman, for it was he who now had the command of HMS Tartar, with Baker having been injured in the head by a falling block, shook his head.

"I am sorry, but we need our boats to deploy kedges... You see... We must get the ship off..."

Kuhlin started to get angry. "Listen, lieutenant, that can wait. Your ship is fine. There are no tides here, so you won't be getting either higher or lower water. You can get off or not get off, whenever you want. But there might be a woman in the water and there is not a minute to be lost. Lower a boat and help searching, now!"

Reeman shook his head slowly. Then he disappeared.

"I can't believe it," Kuhlin growled. Then he ordered the sails to be sheeted in, and the fishing smack started to move, slowly circling the waters around the frigate.

The cold water clutched around her like a giant iron fist. She could not breathe, she could not move, she could not even think. When she surfaced, propelled upwards by the air trapped in her clothes, Anna gasped for air. Blinking away the salt water out of her eyes, she tried to look around her, but she could not move her head. She tried to swim, but she could not move her legs. She still could feel her arms, though, so she tried to move them, to turn herself around. Every move was an immense effort, exhausting her, making her gasp. Slowly she managed to turn around until she saw the ship. It was about fifty yards away. Too far to swim to, she realized. She wondered why she didn't feel cold. Shouldn't she be freezing? Instead she felt almost warm. Her brain was working so slowly, she felt like she was going to fall asleep. Couldn't do that, surely. She would die then, would she not?

She thought about Eric. What would he feel if she died. Would he be angry? Or sad? The thought made her almost smile. She felt a burst of energy, some last effort of her brain... Or was it her heart? She tried to move her arms again, paddling, she even felt her legs, faintly. Concentrating, she tried to move them. But they would not obey.

Anna felt a short sting of despair, then her mind started to drift away. She felt sleepy. Nothing did really matter, did it? And actually, it was quite warm.

Kuhlin knew that their chances of finding Anna alive were minimal. In these temperatures a human body does not survive many minutes. Lots of clothes as well as body fat could prolong the time, but only with a few minutes.

"Eric?" he said softly. af Klint was still sitting on the thwart, head in his hands.

"You are not much help just sitting there," Kuhlin continued.

Eric lifted his head. "I doubt there is anyone who can help now."

Kuhlin nodded. "We must still try."

And they resumed their search. Tapper, standing in the bows, watched the starboard side while the two fishermen kept their lookout to larboard. Kuhlin was at the tiller, steering the boat.

It was, however, Eric who spotted her after all. And not where they would have expected her to be. As he rose from his position on the thwart, finally having overcome the despair that had paralyzed him, he gazed at the British frigate, still aground, but with the damaged rigging now cleared away and boats being prepared to be lowered over the side in order to row out anchors to be used to haul the ship off the ground.

And a little to the right of the ship a white figure stood waist deep in the water. She looked like a ghost, completely unmoving, arms hanging limp down her sides.

MISS ANNA'S FRIGATE

"Oh God! There she is!" Eric screamed.

Anna had barely been conscious when her feet touched the rocks. But the very contact with the solid ground kicked her brain into life again, and she did feel the rocks against her feet, she could move her legs and, finding support, scrambling between strands of seaweed, slipping on wet rock, eventually finding an even surface, she stood there, on a submerged skerry, shivering, but alive, and, vital parts of her body no longer in contact with ice cold water, she was quite a bit farther from death indeed.

When the fishing smack closed the skerry, Anna didn't even react. She just stood there, until Eric jumped into the water himself and carried her back to the boat. He put her into the cabin and covered her with a dirty blanket, while Tapper tried to get the stove going in order to get the temperature up.

"Eh, sorry, sir, but I think you really should get that dress off her," Tapper said.

Eric blushed. "I know, I just thought...," then he realized that Tapper and Anna had been in the sauna together. He snorted. "Ah, well, I guess you have seen it all before... Eh..."

"The stove is burning now, sir, so I will leave you to it," Tapper volunteered, grinning.

As soon as he had left, Eric started to undress the

shivering woman. He then removed his own clothes, discarded the filthy blanket and lay down next to her, pulling his boat cloak over them. Wrapping his arms and legs tightly around her, he held her against him, his face buried in her hair and felt the warmth slowly return to her body.

Epilogue

"She never had a chance to save the king in the first place," Kuhlin explained. He was sitting at his dining table, and so were his wife, bosun Tapper and Karin. Tapper looked into his coffee cup, probably trying to see the bottom in order to verify the right amount of vodka having been added. Karin, her face slightly flushed, tried to behave ladylike, but still couldn't stop herself from peering at the bosun a little too often.

"He never even got close to Norrköping, do you see," Kuhlin continued. "He was seized in the very palace itself, even before general Adlersparre and his rebel troops reached the capital. Which probably was a good thing."

"So there will be no civil war now?" Charlotte asked with relief in her voice.

"No, dear, there will not. The king is securely held at Gripsholm castle and Duke Karl has taken his place for the time being."

"But what about the Russians?"

Kuhlin frowned. "The war, unfortunately, isn't over..."

"But you don't have to go back to those cursed gunboats, do you?" his wife asked.

"No, I don't think so. I'm a commander now, so they will have to give me something bigger. At least a galley, or one of those archipelago frigates." He smiled. "So I will have a real cabin with a bed and a desk at last. And if I'm lucky I will be allowed to choose my own bosun." He winked at Tapper.

The bosun blushed, hastily taking a gulp of his coffee to disguise it.

"I know, Eric," Anna said softly, her hand stroking his back as they lay next to each other, once again in blissful solitude at Eric's estate.

Of course it all had been a stupid idea. She knew that. Perhaps had known it all along. But she really didn't have a chance, did she? And Eric had saved her life once again. She wondered what would happen to Captain Baker. He was such a nice man, and it would be a pity if he would get punished for what was essentially her fault.

"Anna?" Eric asked, then hesitated. "Why did you feel so strongly about helping the king?"

Anna's body tensed for a moment, then relaxed again. She sighed.

"You don't need to tell me...." Eric already regretted having asked. He didn't want to pry into her past or her motives. Not really. But the question had intrigued him nonetheless.

She raised her head and smiled at him. "It's all right, dear. It's just... I don't really know. It might be that when I am getting into something, I commit myself completely. I just must follow it through..."

"Oh."

She looked into his eyes. "I always follow my instincts, Eric. I can't explain why I am acting like I am – not even to myself."

He lifted his hands to her face and took it between them. Then he kissed her softly.

"I think, perhaps, that is what makes you so attractive."

"You think?" she said, her voice throaty.

"Yes," he whispered, resuming his kiss more deeply.

Afterword

This novel is a work of fiction, and it is so to a much higher degree than its prequel, Gunboat Number 14. This needs, perhaps, to be said mostly in defense of poor Captain Baker. He did indeed command HMS Tartar in the Baltic at the time, but there is no evidence he ever disregarded his duty or became besotted with a voluptuous Swedish spy. HMS Tartar never became trapped in the ice either.

The Swedish king, Gustavus IV Adolphus, was indeed removed from his throne in March 1809. There were rebel troops on their way and civil war could have been the result if a group of seven officers, lead by Carl Johan Adlercreutz hadn't acted so swiftly.

Gustavus IV Adolphus was held at Gripsholm castle during the rest of 1809, until he was exiled to Germany. He left Sweden on Christmas Eve aboard our friend, the frigate Camilla.

Camilla was of course never off Norrköping either, there being no king to rescue or British intervention to prevent. She was, however, one of Sweden's most famous frigates ever, a very special design much of which later was imitated by other nations.

Other details I have tried to describe as accurately as possible. Beckens inn really was used by conspirators at the time and there were public bathing houses like the one where Karin works. There were girls like her, too.

As for the weather, the winter of 1809 was a cold one with lots of snow and ice, as was the winter of 2010, when this novel was written.

The Finnish war itself did not end until September 17. There were, however, no more major battles at sea, the fighting mostly taking place in the North of Sweden.

Sweden lost the war and the possession of Finland. As a consequence of the peace treaty, Sweden also turned against Britain, closing its ports to British shipping and formally declaring war. The new Swedish line of kings eventually became French, the Bernadottes, who still remain today.

JENS KUHN

About the prequel

Gunboat Number 14

It's 1808 and Sweden is at war with Russia. The war is not going well. On land, the Swedish army is retreating continuously and all that stands between the Russians and the Swedish mainland are the gunboats of the inshore fleet. The sea war amongst the islands of the Finnish and Swedish archipelagos is a special kind of war, fought in open boats by badly equipped men without proper training. Fighting the weather as much as the Russians, Lieutenant Johan Kuhlin commands a small squadron of three gunboats on special duty. During the short and wet summer, he learns that an independent command isn't all glory and that spies can be more dangerous than Russian guns.

Reader's comments from the blog:

"I loved his book, Gunboat Number 14 - check it out - I dare you not to adore the lovely Anna, and will fight you if you don't."

"If you liked Patrick O'Brian's naval war stories, but wished there was a little more sex sprinkled through them, Gunboat # 14 is the book for you."